COORPAROO BLUES

&

THE IRISH FANDANGO

Coorparoo Blues
&
The Irish Fandango

G. S. MANSON

**DARK
PASSAGE**

A Dark Passage book
Published by Verse Chorus Press
PO Box 14806, Portland OR 97293
info@versechorus.com

Design and layout by Steve Connell/Transgraphic
Dark Passage logo by Mike Reddy

Printed in China

FIRST EDITION

Library of Congress Cataloging-in-Publication data

Manson, G. S., 1965–
  Coorparoo Blues & the Irish Fandango : dark passage / G.S. Manson.
—1st ed.
     p. cm.
   ISBN 978-1-891241-32-1 (pbk.) – ISBN 978-1-891241-89-5 (ebook)
1. World War, 1939-1945—Australia—Fiction. 2. Detectives—Australia—
Fiction. I. Title. II. Title: Coorparoo Blues and the Irish Fandango.
 PR9619.4.M35C88 2012
 823'.92--dc22

                                2012004158

COORPAROO BLUES

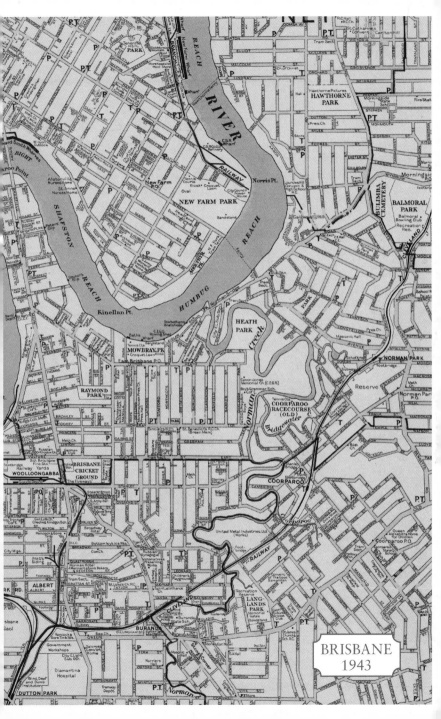

BRISBANE
1943

A glossary of Australian slang can be found at the end of this book

1

FRIDAY

The phone sounded like it was at the bottom of a well, and the Bakelite handle was already hot from sitting in the thin sliver of sun that sliced down between the blind and the window frame. He lifted it to his ear as the woman turned over, taking the soggy sheets with her.

"Hello."

His temples throbbed. Fucking hospital brandy, but what could you do? The bloody Yanks had commandeered every drop of decent grog in town.

"Will you accept a collect call from Melbourne?"

"Don't be silly."

"Caller, the number won't accept . . . No, I can't give him a message . . . Thank you."

He put the receiver back in the cradle.

The bed was like an oven, and with the brown light coming through the hessian it was like sitting at the bottom of a pool of muddy water. As he slid gently away from the snoring form beside him, the phone rang again.

"Mr Munro?"

"I said I won't accept it."

"Accept what?"

It was a different voice, and a lot more interesting. There wasn't that nasal twang the local girls had, which you usually only noticed if you'd been away. This was languid but precise. It had class.

"I'm sorry, I've just hung up from something else."

"I'm sure you have. But I'd like to discuss engaging your services, if I may."

He snapped to.

"Wait a minute, where did you get this number? I've got an office, you know."

She wasn't ruffled.

"Don't bite me, Mr Munro. I'm just in a bit of a hurry, and we've got some mutual friends. Can I come and see you?"

He was still on guard.

"Yeah, at the office. I presume you know where that is, since you're so well informed."

"Of course. In an hour, then?"

A slight breeze in the corridor cooled Jack's feet as he headed to the bathroom. A figure stood by the door, and it wasn't a bad one. She would never have been a beauty queen, but age and a few kids hadn't taken the toll it did on some. She looked after herself. She could afford to.

"Well now, if it isn't Errol Flynn."

"Come on, Vida, a bloke's gotta have his fun while he's young."

"Hah! That's a good one. You won't see forty again."

"I'm only as old as the woman I feel."

"Well I know *that*, don't I. But listen here, Valentino, don't be spreading it too thin. Ya rent's due tomorrow and we're going to the Excelsior for a bit of a knees-up . . . remember?"

"I'll be there."

Her tone hardened.

"And another thing . . . when's your PMG pal putting in that extension? Everyone else here's not too impressed about havin' to walk down to the shops and queue up for the phone, while you lounge around like a lord takin' calls in ya room."

"There's a war on, ya know."

"Only for some."

He kissed her on the cheek in passing, and went into the bathroom.

The cold shower wasn't; you could shave in it. But he was soon back in the room feeling much brighter.

He surveyed the shelf as he ran a comb through his hair. California Poppy – or Crepe Myrtle? Nah, stick with the poppy. This sheila had class; no point smellin' like a nancy boy.

He shook the form in the crumpled bed.

"Righto, love. Time to go."

"Don't I even get a cup of coffee?"

"You been hangin' out with seppoes too much. Make yourself some tea. I'm off; let yaself out."

"Charmed, I'm sure. Aren't you forgetting something?"

"Like what?"

She reached over and picked up her purse from the handbag that lay tangled up in the tatty lingerie on the rug. She opened it up and smiled coyly. "Something for me trouble. And besides, I need new stockings; I've laddered 'em on ya floorboards."

"Wait a bloody minute. I was throwin' money around like confetti last night!"

"Big deal! I can get that off any Yank – and not have to go all the way, neither!"

He leaned over, grabbed her by the hair, and kissed her roughly.

"Yeah, but them young bucks are two-minute shooters any-way. The old bull's got a bit more lift-power, don't ya reckon."

"No complaints there, Jack, but you can't go far on the old army pay while the man's away."

"Don't act like a whore, Betty, or ya might end up one."

Time was a-wasting; Jack tucked a new blue fiver into her purse and grabbed his hat. It was a dark fedora; a Panama would have made more sense in the blazing heat that waited outside, but he didn't want to look like some clown in Africa or somewhere. He threw his coat over his shoulder and went down the rickety steps.

A tram was trundling up Gladstone Road, so he sprang on board before it had stopped, and the clippie gave him a big smile as he rang the bell twice. The drivers always liked that too; it meant they didn't have to drop sand to get started again after pulling up on the steep incline.

He sat in the toast-rack and took in the breeze as they crested the Dornoch Terrace corner and picked up speed heading down Highgate Hill. The river snaked into the haze, and St Andrews loomed up to block the view of town as they rattled past Brisbane State High.

He got off at Cordelia Street and walked down towards South Brissie station. A few black GIs lounged around on the corners, and he saw a knot of them climbing through a tin fence into a backyard in Fish Lane.

"Some bastard must be fleecing 'em with some two-up," he chuckled.

Jack's office sat above a fruit shop, and as he headed up the stairs between it and the bootmaker's, Leo the owner waved.

"Gotta visitor, mister Jack! She pretty nice, I reckon."

"No flies on me." The voice echoed down the stairwell.

She sat outside the office door, fanning herself with the arvo *Telegraph*.

Shit, was it that late in the day?

As he opened the office, she looked up at him through the blonde silken fall of her Veronica Lake cut. Every second woman wore it these days, but few as well as this.

"On time to the minute, Mr Munro. I like that in a man."

This one knew what she was worth. She sat perched in the chair like a Myer's model.

"Call me Jack."

"Very well, Jack. I want you to find my husband."

"You're not wearing a ring."

"Very observant. We are separated."

"Don't wanna cruel the pitch, eh?"

"That was crude and uncalled for. I expected better from you."

"Did you? How come?"

"I've been told that you are a discreet and effective operator, Mr Munro, if a bit rough around the edges and rather too eager for a quid. So I'll overlook your rather base view of my circumstances. Now, will you find my husband for me or not?"

He sat back, impressed.

"The umpire would call that a six, lady."

"And I can keep batting all afternoon if I need to," she shot back.

She was as cool as a gunbarrel, and just as dangerous.

"Who'd he run off with then?"

"I imagine that your clientele are usually concerned with matters below the belt, but this is a simple missing persons case."

The word simple rang alarm bells. It usually meant the opposite.

"The police?"

A bead of sweat appeared on her forehead, and he knew

there was more to this than met his bloodshot eye this steamy afternoon. He turned on the desk fan and angled it toward her.

"I see."

"Do you, Mr Munro?"

"I see someone who needs to give me some more details before I get involved."

"Ah, I'm afraid not. You must accept the case before I tell you any more."

That was like a red rag.

"Okay, I'm in," he said, trying not to stare at her cleavage as it started to gleam in the humid confines of the office.

"Excellent. Here is a photo of my husband. His name is Reginald Flowers. He came up here from Melbourne to meet with some associates two weeks ago, and I haven't heard a thing since."

The photo was a studio job, not a happy snap, and the subject was definitely some sort of spiv, Ronald Colman mo and all.

"What's his line of business?"

"Import and export."

"And who was he meeting?"

"Some American gentlemen."

Dust motes curled lazily in the fan's wake.

"They wouldn't be military gentlemen, would they, by any chance? Acting in, let's say, an unofficial capacity?"

"I'm sure I couldn't say. Perhaps."

The word was loaded with more than it could carry. She brushed back her hair and looked right into his eyes.

"Anyway, that's for you to find out, isn't it?"

She threw a card on the table.

"I'll be staying at this establishment. They are discreet, and you can contact me there at any time, day or night."

As she walked out the door, she turned with a look that

would stretch the strides of any man.

"I *can* count on you, can't I?"

"With all ya fingers, love."

With that she was gone. Moments later, he realised they hadn't even discussed a fee. Well, that could wait till they next met . . . and who knew what goodies might come to light before it was time to settle up?

He wheeled the chair back, bent down and lifted the rug, then prised up a floorboard and took his Colt 45 from its hiding place. He was no stranger to the black market: there were some rum individuals involved.

Still, it beat crawling around the New Guinea jungle like some poor bastards. Thank God they were, though, and good luck to them, coward or hero. But he'd seen enough mud in the last show, so that King 'n' Country stuff rang a bit hollow now. Anyway, off to turn over a couple of lurk merchants and see what crawled out.

2

As the tram trundled past the desolate spot where the great Cathedral of the Holy Name was supposed to have been built, Jack saw knots of men standing around drinking and smoking. They'd be in the pews themselves, he thought, if the Archbishop hadn't decided to send the money to Rome to be blessed. The priest entrusted with the task promptly took off for Rio with the dosh . . . Fucken dills, he laughed to himself.

He got off at Brunswick Street and strolled up the hill past McWhirter's, then round the corner to the Waterside Workers Hall, opposite Warner Street. A big man stood at the door in shirtsleeves.

His tattooed arms were like sides of beef, and he wasn't pretty.

"Lenny in?"

"Fuck off, this is a private do."

"Look, I'm not here to drink ya precious piss, I just wanna talk to Len."

"You deaf, mate?"

A short man with glasses appeared.

"What's the trouble?"

"No trouble, can ya just pop up the stairs and tell Lenny that the Mower's here."

The functionary tootled back up while the big man scowled at Jack.

"Where'd ya get that silly fucken moniker?"

"'Cause I spend most of me time in people's backyards."

"And mowin' their fucken grass too! So keep an eye on ya missus!" came a booming voice. "He's sweet, let 'im in."

He pushed past the bouncer and shook Lenny's hand with a firm grip.

"How are they hangin', digger."

"One each side of the seam, mate."

Lenny and Jack went back a long way. They'd met while convalescing in Blighty after the last big German push on the Western Front petered out, and as soon as they were both mobile again, they'd spent a great deal of time chasing skirt up and down Piccadilly's back streets. They weren't from the same unit, but they'd been close enough in the line to not have to bother discussing the finer points of war, and both being pants men of the first water, they'd not missed out on much in the immediate post-war celebrations.

They'd lost track of each other after coming back in '19, and next met over a picket line in central Queensland during the big sugar strike in '35. Len just appeared one day at the mill; he was obviously not some swaggie, had to be there delivering or gathering intelligence for the union.

Jack was one of the local coppers; he knew it had been decided to break the strike by force and target the organisers for some serious tap-dancing in the cells. He didn't know what had turned Len into a commo, but he wasn't about to stand by and see an old mate kicked into imbecility if he could help it. The night before the planned action, he took off his badge, crept down to the camp and gave him the mail.

Len was no fool. The bulls had his number – some bastard had shopped him – and he was done for if they nabbed him. Their meeting was tense, but Jack slipped him a few quid to be going on with, as well as some tea and baccy. They shook on it, and Len was on the first rattler going south.

Jack was dobbed in by some pimp in the camp, and next morning got a very serious rocket under him from the inspector who'd come up to sort out the show. Too bad: what was done was done. He might have permanently blotted his copybook with the force, but he'd stood by his cobber, politics aside, and that's all a man *can* do if he wants to stand up straight in God's clean sunlight.

He hadn't gone all bloody fascist like a lot of returned men who copped it raw after they came back and the welcome home had worn off. But a man's beliefs were his own business, and not to be discussed at the table, as they say.

These days Len and Jack had the odd beer down in Fortitude Valley, where Len kept court in several watering holes, and swapped yarns about various goings-on around town. They were good sources for each other, and widely regarded to be as thick as thieves.

There was a ding-dong party in progress at the top of the grimy stairs: the whole floor was full of shirt-sleeved wharfies hoeing into plates of prawns carried around by some very buxom sorts: totally topless, with barely a bit of twine and hanky covering up the best bit. There was a line of kegs gushing forth the sauce, and on a trestle table a stripper was going the whole hog with a beer bottle as a projector showed some grainy old donkey show on the back wall. It was on for young 'n' old, and the din was deafening.

They grabbed their drinks and went back to the rear of the

room, where the big windows looked out over the dull red roofs and down to the river at Teneriffe.

"Left the missus at home then, Len?"

"No, she's up on stage, ya clown."

They cackled into the frothy heads of their beers.

"So what's happening Jack, ya prick."

He palmed the photo over.

"Lookin' for this cove. He's a bit swish, but into the odd lurk."

Len's face darkened.

"Ya won't find *him*, mate."

"Why, you seen 'im?"

"Once or twice."

"And?"

"He's been naughty, and he's no longer around as far as I know."

"Meaning?"

"Meaning whatever you want it to."

"Come on, you can do better than that for an old digger."

"Mate, a word to the wise: Don't look too hard. Who wants him?"

"His missus."

"What's she look like then?"

"Very tasty."

"Settle for that, mate. Spiel her some shit, grab the mun, and then try ya luck. Trust me, stay away from this one. It's smelly."

"Mate, I gotta keep up appearances . . . What's the story?"

A long silence.

"Okay, but don't blame me if it bites ya. He was doing a bit of backdoor stuff with some darkies on the other side of the river."

"What, Abos?"

"No, ya mug. Tan Yanks . . . spooks!"

"They got their own game goin'?"

"Some have, and from what I gather there was some disagreement about dodgy goods. So Flash Harry here comes up from down south, kicks up a stink, then next thing he's gone, and it wasn't back home, they tell me. So you work it out. Ya want my advice, make up some guff for his wife, and then go fishin'."

"Are the cops on to it?"

"Don't know, don't care. And why would they fucken tell me?"

He drained the glass.

The conversation was over, and Jack took the cue.

"Mate, I'd love to stick around, but . . ."

"Mate, will ya be told? Leave it alone. Look, we're rafflin' off the tarts later, I'll fix the draw for ya."

He could tell a hollow offer when he heard it.

"Nah mate, she's right. I emptied the bag last night – and I got work to do."

"Suit yaself."

"I'll catch ya."

He hit the street coughing slightly. Smoky rooms got to him quickly. It had only been a touch of the gas, not enough to take him out of the line for long, but enough for it to hang around shitting him ever since – a regular reminder of how precious a thing it can be to breathe.

The streets were filling up with gangs of Aussies on the lookout for a fuck or a fight, and preferably both. Things had calmed down since the big dust-up at the PX in Edward Street a couple of months back, but the Yanks still had it all over the Diggers in pay and clobber, so trouble was easy to find if you wanted it.

Even though it was as good as dark, Jack could feel the heat of the day still coming off the big wall at All Hallow's as he strolled back into town. There'd be a breeze off the river down near the National, but he couldn't wait. A tram came clacketing up behind him, he hailed it, and it slowed down enough for him to leap on. The clippie didn't even approach him for the fare, just nodded, and kept looking out to the west with a faraway gaze: what memories of his were going down with that last glimpse of the sun, and what horrors rising with it on the other side of the world?

3

There was only one bloke worth talking to if you wanted to know who'd been doing what on the dodgy side of the river: Soupy Jones. No-one knew where his nickname came from, but the Soup had his fingers into everything: SP, knocking shops, sly grog, hot property, and god knows what else besides. He had so many of the rozzers in his pocket, his strides wouldn't hold up. He held court at the Majestic Hotel off Stanley Street, and it wasn't the place for a G&T after tennis. They still had sawdust on the floor to mop up the spilt beer, piss, and blood – and it wasn't changed daily.

It was after seven, so the doors would be shut to the general citizenry, but the place would still be going full tilt with the lights on, in plain view of the occasional passing police officer who'd ostentatiously ignore what was going on inside.

He'd had a few dealings with the Soup, but no run-ins, and that was a good thing. The bastard weighed at least three hundred pounds and settled most physical altercations by launching his enormous bulk straight at his opponent, flattening them against the nearest wall or piece of furniture, then sitting on them with all the downward force he could muster. That was usually enough. Men were reputed to have died as a result of this procedure, and ruptured organs were a common outcome. One enterprising young hoon had shot him three times in a spat over some doxy the Soup had defiled, but the bullets all lodged in the blubber which engirdled him, and the fat one merely ended up with some ugly bruises. The rumour was, he escaped gangrene or any other infection because his blood was toxic enough to kill all known germs. The fate of the young Romeo was also the stuff of legend: he hanged himself after finding that his true love had returned to the embrace of the fat man (and friends), preferring material comforts and a life of dissolution to the promised transports of true romance.

The spivvy young cockatoo at the side door of the pub was an unfamiliar addition to the Soup's gang. There was no point in Jack trying to talk his way in, so he nipped down the alley behind the old three-storey building and cased the back lane. The corrie fence had been cut into spear points with tinsnips, and the brick wall that ran down the side of the dunny run was topped with cemented glass and barbed wire. I've gone over worse than that, he laughed to himself.

He looked around; the rubbish bins were all full of putrid scraps and offal, but there were plenty of sacks of dead marines out for the bottle-o. One was barely a quarter full. That'd do nicely.

He squatted on his heels and removed the bottles as gently as possible. Softly softly, he thought, as he lined up the last bottle with the others at the foot of the gate; they would slow down any unforeseen pursuers should he have to leave that way later.

He grabbed the spud bag, folded it in half, then climbed up on one of the bins and laid it over the brick wall. Grabbing a rock, as quietly as possible he hammered down any sharp protuberances under the sacking. Then he was over the wall in seconds, landing like a cat, his soft shoes making no sound on the paved yard.

He waited a second till his eyes adjusted to the light, then moved a packing case over to that spot, in case he needed a quick exit and could do the Spring-heeled Jack routine back over into the alley. The back door was unlocked, and he sauntered through the pisser and into the pub as if he'd been there all day.

The whole room was a sea of hats. The swearing, laughing, arguing, and general bonhomie didn't hide the fact that this was a fairly rough crew, who were there by dint of their complete disregard for the law. Any half-decent copper could have signed off on a year's worth of cases by locking the doors and arresting the lot. But that wouldn't happen while the Soup ran the show.

The boss wasn't down in the bar; Jack would have to beard him in his den. He walked up the stairs to the room where the fat one would be holding court if he was in. He was. He sat bulging behind a desk, wearing green eyeshades, while a tart with not much on lolled about on the sofa under the window. Rat-faced underlings leaned against the walls in a haze of blue smoke, hanging on every word from the puckered hole in Soup's greasy jowls.

Jack got off the mark first.

"Soup, you old bludger, gettin' a bit?"

"Every day, bastard face. Where'd you spring from?"

"Round 'n' about."

"How'd ya get in here? You're not on my Christmas list."

"I'm hurt to hear ya say that about an old mate, Soup, really I am."

"Cut the codswallop, whattya want?"

Before Jack could answer, the fat man turned to one of his lieutenants: "Go downstairs and give that clown Ed a smack in the chops – straight up without warning. Then send 'im up here, you relieve 'im on the door, and do ya fucken job properly."

"That's a bit harsh, isn't it?"

"I run a tight ship, Munro, as you well know, and if a tired old bugger like you can slip past my defences and get on board, what chance have I got against some more determined party with grievous intent."

"Good point. Anyway, I'm just here checking if you've seen some dill from down south whose missus seems to have lost him."

"How would I know where a respectable married man would be?"

This was a huge joke to all present; it took a while for the general guffawing to die down.

"Because he fancies himself as a bit of a lurk merchant, and he may well have trespassed on your patch, heaven forbid."

He flipped the photo onto the desk.

The Soup gave nothing away.

"Never seen him in me life."

"You sure?"

"My word not good enough for ya, Munro?"

"It just seems unlikely that this joker would be doing what he was doing and you wouldn't know about it, given that he was supposed to have been skiving around this area."

The tone never changed; the fat one was too clever for that.

"Are you seriously suggesting I had something to do with his disappearance?"

"What, an upstanding citizen like yourself?"

The ice came into his demeanour.

"No-one likes a smart-alec, Munro. If I were you, I'd go back to creeping 'round catching housewives copping one off the butcher."

He stood up just as the cockatoo from downstairs walked in

rubbing his jaw.

Soup exploded at him.

"Did you let this cunt in?"

"Umm . . . no."

"Well you fucken imbecile, what's he doing here?"

"Umm . . . I dunno."

"Jesus, Mary and fucken Joseph! I pay you to watch a door, right? And yet this joker just strolls in like the Duke of Windsor, and you don't know how. Fucken clown! Ya docked next week's pay, and ya got no visiting rights with the girls for a month. Maybe a bit of pullin' ya puddin' might sharpen your eyesight. Now get out."

Jack couldn't resist.

"Wouldn't it do the opposite?"

The fat man turned; he wasn't amused.

"You too. I don't wanna see your rough head for a long time. Now piss off while I'm still in a good mood."

As they went down the stairs the young doorman snarled, "You're gone, pal. I'll get you for this."

Jack laughed.

"You'll have to get up a bit earlier, chum. I was puttin' it over mugs like you before you were even swimmin' in your old man's bag. Don't take it personally."

He went out onto the street, glad to be away from the fuggy smell of beer, smoke and sweat, and started walking back towards the office. Before he got fifty yards from the pub, he heard the sound of bottles rattling over the cobbles in the darkness behind him. There was no way Soup was going to let it drop without finding out what Jack knew . . . He had a tail.

Jack kept a steady pace as he crossed Grey Street, picking it up as he went down Russell Street into the tunnel. The columns holding up the railway bridge gave the huge dark cavern a Gothic feel, like some mossy old cathedral ruin, and the headlights of a solitary vehicle lit up the squadrons of pigeons that nested up in the grimier reaches of the ceiling. When he got about halfway along the passage, he slowed down until he was clear of the cones of light from the few light bulbs that worked, then quickly jumped behind one of the pillars and squatted down in the dark, well below the eye-height of anyone following, and waited. The tentative steps behind him crunched slowly closer as his shadow tried to work out where he'd got to. Sure enough, as the figure drew level with him he saw the man had a small pistol in his hand. His pursuer was warily casing the area, but not looking into the dark shadows to the left of his feet.

Jack leapt up and chopped down on the man's wrist, making the gun go off with a sharp crack. He twisted it out of the man's hand, head-butted him, then whipped out his own piece and pointed it at the man's face.

"Not you again! What's this fucken popgun?"

It was a short .22 pistol – no cannon, but dangerous enough in experienced hands . . . which it wasn't.

"Shit!" said the youth."He'll kill me now."

"Not if I get in first . . . Not your day, is it?"

"Please, mate, let me go. Don't give us up."

The bravado was all gone; it was a scared kid looking up at him.

"You milkbar gangsters are all the same. Learn to fight with ya fists before you carry one of these things, in case ya lose it . . . like now."

"I seen that guy," the snivelling youth proffered in the latest style.

"Have you now? What *guy*?"

"The one you're looking for. That's why Soupy sent me after

ya. I seen him there at the pub a few times."

"You wouldn't be making this up to get off detention, would ya?"

"No, four square! I seen him at Murgon Mary's too; he was selling pills and stuff."

"What pills?"

"You know, the wake-up gear . . . for the girls and the truckies that call in. And stuff like that."

"When was this?"

"Week or two back. He came in and there was lots of argy-bargy with Soup, and some Yanks as well. That's all I know, mister. I was on the door all the time, honest."

"Alright, young feller me lad, where are you from?"

"Toowoomba."

"Why didn't you take the King's shilling? Why are you running round with crooks and sluts and molls instead of defending us against the heathen Jappo?"

"Tuberculosis and flat feet."

Fair enough.

"Righto, you go back to my mate Soup and tell him I went back to the office. Then you lose yourself, mate. Piss off back to Mum."

"Mum's dead."

"Very well then, ya bloody auntie. I don't care, I just don't want to see you round here again. If I do, ya won't get off so light."

He emptied the chambers of the .22 and handed it back.

"They'll miss this. Give it back and go home."

The kid grabbed it and bolted. Jack winced as he turned to leave; his old footy knees hurt from squatting down. Bloody hell, who was he: the Salvos? What a caper. Anyway, Murgon Mary's wasn't too far away – and what was another smelly brothel? It was gunna be a long night.

The two-storey mansion would have been one for the nobs in the old days, but it had sunk in tone with the rest of the neighbourhood. There were holes in the balusters, and paint was an unknown concept to whoever rented it out to the madam. Mary was a tough customer: she had to be to survive running a knocking shop in this part of town. Now that the black GIs were confined to this side of the river, they went there in droves, and no respectable white man would be seen knocking on the old lead-lighted doors.

Mary was dark herself, but that was reputedly due to Afghan rather than Aboriginal blood, and she had none of the resigned deference to white conventions and society that a lot of the blackfellers had. No nonsense was the rule at her establishment, and even rough-house sailors doffed their caps on entry. The girls were all "exotic" as well, and word had it that the room downstairs with covered-up windows was a den of white slavers indulging in opium orgies to their heart's content. It was a good place to get stabbed, whatever your social standing.

As Jack crossed the timber walkway which led to the ground floor, he could see lights down in the basement, which was below street level. As he wondered about the reputed goings-on within, a callow, mean-faced figure approached. This one was young too, but more sure of himself, probably late twenties and brought up rough. The arms that stuck out of the vest he wore over his singlet were stringy and tanned. He had the poise of a fighter, and bad manners.

"What's your game, sport?"

"I'm here to see the boss lady."

"She's not working these days."

"This is business."

"I doubt it."

"Look, mate, I just want a quick word and I'm off, fair enough?"

"Show me ya money."

"What for?"

"'Cause you aren't here for any hanky panky, which means I don't get me percentage. So you pay me for me trouble, then piss off."

"That's a raw deal."

"It's the only one goin', old man. Now cough up."

"How 'bout you just be a good boy and go get the boss and stop playing silly buggers."

"You had ya chance," he shot back (which is something you should never tell them), hauling out a razor as quick as a flash.

Jack was ready. He threw his right arm in the air and wiggled his fingers, taking the hood's glance up with them, then drove his right knee up into the man's solar plexus. Whipping off his hat to cover the blade, he swung his elbow into the side of the man's face, dislocating his jaw, then hauled him around, pulled out the Colt, lashed him about the scone three or four times, and flipped the limp form over the railing, where it landed with a crash in the clump of banana trees below.

His blood was up.

He stormed down the verandah and kicked open the front door with the Colt held high. The girl at the desk screamed when she saw the gun.

"Shut up, moll!" he yelled, then headed down the corridor. Various heads popped out of doorways, then straight back in again when they saw the gun and the wild-eyed figure holding it.

He got to the main room. Two girls were already fleeing with their customers as a man came out of the kitchen holding a carving knife.

"Drop it or die, mate."

He pointed the gun at the half-dressed patron, who did as he was told, just as Mary walked into the room and stopped. She was dressed very well, but that didn't disguise a hard operator. He'd seen brown snakes who looked more friendly.

"What the fuck's this?" she demanded.

"A bloke who's run out of patience with all you fucken low-lifes bullshitting me, that's who. Now get over here and sit down before I shoot some bastard!"

"Johnny!" she yelled.

"I think you'll find him down in the yard with the garbage."

She stiffened and backed off to stand against the wall, beside a table on which sat an unopened half bottle of good scotch, abandoned by the fleeing couples.

He threw the photo down.

"This prick . . . the story . . . *now*. Who is he?"

She tried to take control of the situation.

"You look excited, mate. You need to calm down."

"Listen, love, you could be smokin' my peg with a mouthful of ice, and I'd still be steamed up. Now I know he was dealin' in truck lollies and what have ya, so answer the bloody question."

She didn't need much nous to see he was in a troublesome mood, and went along with it.

"Righto. It's Reg somethin' or other. He sold us some stuff . . . it was rubbish. The bastard wouldn't give us the dough back, then some other jokers threatened him as well, and he just vanished. Done a runner, I'll wager. So I'm still outta pocket, and I don't need this malarkey from you, whoever ya are, alright? That's it. Anything else?"

"Where did he get it from?"

"How would I know? But they were useless, utter shit. Now,

that's all ya getting here tonight. Piss off."

"Anyone else know his whereabouts?"

She looked at him askance, as if deciding how to play the hand, and came down on the side of expedience.

"Well, he was fond of one of the girls out at Jessie's place at Coorparoo, that's all I can tell ya."

A siren sounded outside, approaching.

A smirk livened up her angry expression, and she started to walk forward, a lot more confident.

"That'll be for you."

Jack leaned over and grabbed the scotch, pocketed it and the gun, and took off down the back stairs.

Another back fence loomed before him . . . it was the story of his life.

4

He got off the Camp Hill tram at the Kirkland Avenue shops and walked down Ames Street past the pottery. The low-slung buildings glowed from within as the kilns belched smoke into a sky that now looked even more threatening. It was as humid as buggery. The regular arvo thunderstorm had failed to drop its load on the town to cool it all off, and the air was electric with menace.

The strong smell of frangipani wafted about as he strolled up Pembroke Road. It was quiet, and he could see a couple of Negro soldiers ahead of him picking up the pace. I'll just follow these jokers, he thought. They'll know the way.

The house stood at the bottom of a hill and didn't look too different from any of the others in the area, but the figures leaning on the fence and lurking under the awning of the butcher shop two doors up marked it as no ordinary dwelling. As he walked through the gate and across the lawn, a few of the Negroes chiacked him.

"Wrong way, man!"

"You lost, white boy?"

He ignored them. Heading up the stairs he could hear a loud, wooden thumping.

Holy hell! Some bugger must be reefing it in. He'll push the headboard through the wall.

As he got to the top, the biggest man he'd ever seen appeared – a sergeant, and obviously a force to be reckoned with.

"You in the wrong place, mister."

"I go where I like, mate."

"Not here you don't. Now back off down them stairs the easy way."

Jack opened his jacket and pulled out the half bottle of scotch, making sure the big bloke saw the gun tucked into his waistband.

"Look, Sambo, I'm not here for trouble. I'm just looking for a feller might have been around here recently. Okay?"

Whisky speaks any language.

"You call me Sergeant King, feller, and you just behave, so I don't have to get all excited and hurt ya none."

"Fair enough, *Sergeant* King, let's be cobbers, eh? We'll have a nip of this together."

He pushed into the living room. It was pretty tatty: a half dozen black soldiers lounged about, and a few girls decorated a large shabby couch – mostly half-castes, but a couple of slatternly white girls who were definite roughheads made up the numbers. They had that sucked-in face of the Depression years – cheeks hollowed out by a diet of spuds and lard – and they sucked on their gaspers as they checked him out with the hollow eyes of the brutal and desperate. Not his type at all.

"You after some pussy?" said the sergeant.

"Not tonight, chief."

He had nothing against dusky maidens on principle. He spent a whole week in a French brothel full of statuesque Senegalese girls once, and a good time was had by all – but there was work to be done.

He could see now where the thumping had come from.

A young Negro soldier sat in the corner with a guitar, singing some sort of music he'd never heard before and stamping his foot to keep time. Along with the beat there was a weird cater-wauling sound he got by sliding a beer-bottle neck on his finger up and down the fretboard.

Jack was transfixed. What was *this*?

He was no musical dunce: he could still cut a rug, and he kept up with the latest bands to a fair degree. He was a regular at the Troc, when he could manage it, and he liked Glenn Miller (well who didn't); he even had a few Al Bowlly sides at home. Pity about Al copping it in the Blitz – what a loss, the poor bastard sang like a bird.

But this was different. It had a raw, keening sound that really got to him. At first it sounded closer to what you might hear tom-cats doin' on a roof, but if you listened, it was tuneful al-right, and went right through ya. The only thing he could think of like that was bagpipes: they sounded awful until you heard them the right way: like a lone piper one night on a parapet in France, skirling out a lament after the Highlanders had taken a shellacking . . . It went right into the soul of every man on either side of the wire, and not a shot was heard for hours afterwards. This sound came from somewhere like that. It was mournful but urgently alive . . . It sort of scared him.

When the song was finished he went over to the soldier.

"Mate, what *is* that you're playing?"

"That's the blues."

He'd heard the word in a hundred tunes, but they didn't sound like this.

"What sort of blues? I never heard that sound before."

"The blues is whatever you want. It just comes out."

"Who taught ya that stuff?"

"My daddy sang it most days after he'd finish behind the plough. We didn't have no radio."

"The bottle thing, how's that?"

"That's what my daddy did. I dunno where it's from, I just do it."

"Well it fucken sounds alright to me. Who writes it?"

"Anybody."

"What, you write it?"

"I just make up the words; the blues is a feelin'."

"Look, what's your name?"

"Leroy."

"Okay, Leroy, I'm just a dumb white feller here."

"You a cracker, man." He laughed.

"Whatever ya reckon . . . Just run it past me again. How do you just make up a song on the spot?"

Leroy picked up the guitar from his lap.

"Okay, what's this place man? Coo-paroo?"

"Last time I looked."

He began playing.

Well I woke up this mornin' . . . had them Coorparoo blues
Yes I woke up this mornin' . . . had them Coorparoo blues
My baby done left me
Do' know what to do

The slide roared up and down the neck as the rest of the soldiers in the room clapped along and shouted jive talk encouragement.

Well the Coorparoo blues . . . they like holes in yo shoes
Coorparoo blues . . . they like holes in yo shoes
Ain't nothin' left to do
Find me some pussy down Coorparoo

He executed a little flourish of chords, and slapped the body of the guitar as the rest of the room shouted out, "That's it, Leroy!" "You cuttin' it, man!"

Jack was stunned by the power and simplicity of it. He dragged a mouthful out of the bottle, then wiped it with his sleeve and handed it to the man with the guitar.

"Is that all there is to it? Well, I'll be fucked."

The young soldier looked strangely bashful, as if he'd never been asked the question before.

"Thassit man, that's how it is. The blues is whatever you got: your pain, your joy, whatever, man. You sing it."

"I'm converted, mate. Can ya get discs of that stuff?"

"Sure, but they ain't too common here. They done some recordin' down Mississippi, and you can git 'em, but we can't hardly afford that kinda shit, so I just do my own. I'm hopin' to make me a record when I get home; it might take me up to Chicago or somewhere."

"That's great stuff, mate. Good on ya!"

Jack didn't give out praise lightly, but this kid sure had the God-given talent, and knew how to use it. The scotch was soon out of his hands and off round the room, so he went over to the couch and sat down next to one of the girls. He showed her the picture as Leroy started up again.

"Anyway, have *you* seen this bloke?"

"Yeah he's been around . . . but not this week. He was causin' trouble and Jessie told him to stay away."

Speak of the devil. A large woman in a drab housecoat and beat-up hat came through the door.

"Who are you, ya bastard."

"Settle down, Jess. The Soup sent me over."

"Oh yeah? Need a bit of chocolate milk, do ya?"

"I'm lookin' for this Reggie dill."

"Well ya won't find 'im here."

"Why not?"

Before she could reply a young soldier burst in yelling: "MPs! MPs!"

The sergeant grabbed Jack by the collar and growled, "You beat it now, man!" before propelling him to the back door and straight down the stairs.

The jeep screeched to a halt at the front gate, and Jack heard boots thumping along the front verandah as he shinned over the back fence and landed in a chook yard. It was as black in there as the arse of the devil himself, so he stood there quietly, figuring he'd make too much noise if he went galumphing over tin fences in the dark. Best to lie doggo and see what transpired.

It sounded nasty. There was a lot of swearing and yelling as well as a general commotion, then the back door flew open and Leroy came hurtling down the stairs followed by two MPs, one of them holding his guitar. A shaft of light from the open door lay across the backyard.

"Who was this white feller, boy?"

"I dunno sir. He jes' liked my music."

"That's horseshit, boy. Yew lyin'!"

"No sir, honest!"

As Jack peeped through a hole in the fence, the tall one turned and smashed the guitar against the tankstand, then threw the splintered mess near the head of the prostrate figure.

"That'll be yo spine, nigger, if you don't tell me the truth."

He stretched out Leroy's hand and started grinding it with his boot.

"Talk, you asshole, or you ain't never gonna play no jungle music never again."

"He was lookin' for some white guy, I don't know! Honest,

he talked to the girls, man. Ask them!"

"Was it Baxter?"

"Who Baxter, man?"

The baton came down hard on Leroy's ribs as they pinned him to the ground.

Jack didn't like watching this sort of stuff from cover, like a dingo, but it was getting tricky; if he jumped out waving a gun at cops, whatever their hue, he might end up in the big house.

He stayed put.

The tall one stood back swinging his club and smacking it into his palm.

"If we find out you know where that nigger-lovin' piece of shit is hidin' out, you a dead man like your two buddies, that clear?"

"I dunno no Baxter, man, I swear."

The MPs stood up.

"Ok let's go shake up them whores in there, see what they know."

The tall one gave one more twist of his heel that made the kid cry out, then both stamped up the stairs.

Leroy lay there whimpering, and Jack could hear more aggravation and slamming of doors in the house before the MPs got back into their jeep and roared off.

The sergeant had come down by the time he was over the fence and crouching beside Leroy.

"Miserable bastards," Jack said, and meant it. American MPs had a bad name, and now he could see why.

"Why don't you beat it, man," said the sergeant. "You caused enough trouble."

"Hey listen, you got enough trouble without *me* around, mate. Who are those pricks . . . and who's Baxter."

"They's the two that shot our buddies."

"What? When?"

"Jes' last week. Oscar and Moses. Those two took 'em down the railway line over there aways and shot 'em, man. Jes' like that."

Jack had heard rumours of such things, but never anything so definite.

"Bullshit."

"No bullshit, man. Some gal went to the MPs and said those two boys done raped her, so they picked 'em up from our depot and took 'em down near that playin' field by the tracks and shot 'em in the haid jes' like they was dogs."

"Who was the girl?"

"We dunno, man . . . and like, they would rape some white piece of ass? No way! Moses was a religious man, with a wife an' all. And Oscar, well, he liked his poontang, but he could get all he wanted right here at Jessie's, no problem. I don't believe none of that shit they said."

"Was there an investigation?"

The sergeant laughed.

"Where you been, you dumb cracker? They can kill us and they don't give a goddamn, just like back home in the land of the free. Wake up, man. Welcome to the Klan."

"First I've heard of it goin' on here, and it don't sit right with this old soldier, for one. And who's Baxter?"

"Some southern boy gone AWOL. He was pretty friendly with the culluds on the ship, and he jes' disappeared when they docked here. They seem to think some of our guys is lookin' out for him while he's loose."

"I think you know more than you're tellin', boss, but you take my card here, and if it should fall on the ground and get picked up by anybody called Baxter, well that'd be coincidence."

"Who *are* you, man?"

"I'm what you'd probably call a private eye."

"I thought I could smell the law on you."

"Me and the law don't have a lot to do with each other, but me and what's right still talk. This whole caper is smellier than prawns gone off in the sun. I don't like it."

"There's a lot we don't like, man, but we gotta wear it."

"We'll see what we can do about that."

He leaned down and patted Leroy on the shoulder as he sat holding his fingers.

"No promises, mate, but if I get a chance to even things up for what those pricks did, don't worry, I'll take it. It's just not manly. Wreckin' those hands is like breakin' a nice vase. I'll see ya 'round."

He turned to the sergeant. "One last question."

"Shoot."

"What are you blokes actually doin' here? I mean, in this area. Aren't most of your units out Darra way?

We're in the Quartermaster's Corps. We got a depot full of medical supplies down there near the station."

"Righto then."

5

Jack hopped over another fence and headed up a driveway onto Hipwood Avenue, then up over the hill. It was getting close to midnight, but there was a chance the local copper would still be up bashing the typewriter. He turned down the street and quickened his step as he saw a light burning in the back room of the residence next to the weatherboard lock-up.

He mounted the stairs and rapped hard on the front door of the office till the light went on at the front desk.

"G'day."

"It's nighttime, mate."

"Yeah well. You'd be Flanagan, wouldn't ya?"

"I would, and you are?"

"Munro."

"O yeah, heard of you. Left under a cloud or somethin'. Bent, weren't ya?"

"No, I wasn't."

That was a laugh, he'd been anything but. Too upright in fact. There was no fruit on the sideboard in his poky little rented house, but he had a family and they loved each other. The missus was cute and pretty cluey, and took in a bit of ironing when the little feller was at school.

They were nothing fancy, unlike the drunken fool in the Bentley who ran over his son one night as he came back from the shops with some milk. The bastard just kept going, leaving the poor little beggar dead in the gutter, and a family in pieces. The rich kid who'd done it turned up at Central next morning with not only the biggest lawyer in the state, but a Chief Inspector as well, to ice the cake.

Nothing ever happened beyond the offer of a bit of hush money he told them to shove. The whole thing was swept under the carpet like a bit of dust by a lazy maid. His kid was dead, his missus in the madhouse, and he was supposed to uphold law 'n' order for these bastards? His whole reason for being a copper was now a black joke, his son's life not worth a squirt of piss. It wasn't good enough.

He took sick leave, and waited. He caught the toff outside a party in a leafy street out Bardon way, and kicked his balls to paste. If he wasn't to have a son, then neither would this ponce. It was a bad business: the fellow ended up in a chair, pissing through a tube for the rest of his natural, and Jack was arse-holed from the force. They couldn't charge him, because then it would all have come out, so it was agreed behind closed doors that enough was enough. He was a marked man from then on, as far as the brass were concerned, but a lot of the footsloggers felt he'd done the only thing left open to him in the circumstances. So they turned a blind eye to his activities, even if the big boys were always on the lookout for an excuse to run him in . . .

But bent? Fuck this Irish fool. He let it go through to the keeper.

"Anyway, I've just heard about some shooting round here recently, where a couple of them black doughboys got chopped."

"Didja now?"

"Sure did."

"What's it to ya?"

"Just interested."

"Well I'm not, and neither should you be."

"Like that, is it?"

"Mate, between you and me, what the Yanks do with their darkies is none of our business."

"Crime's crime, isn't it?"

"It'd be a bigger crime if Tojo and his mates were runnin' down Queen Street rootin' our women and shootin' our kids, which is what would happen if the Yanks weren't here. For my money, they can do what they bloody like if it stops me havin' to dig a foxhole in me front yard."

"Then what about Baxter? Who's Baxter?"

The sergeant smiled.

"More coons?"

"No, a white man apparently."

Flanagan leaned forward.

"Righto, what's this in aid of?"

"Look. Jimmy Simpson said to tell you to tell me what you can, alright?"

Jim was virtually the only high-ranking copper that would still talk to him. They'd both been on a murder up in the scrub and solved it in short order, and they'd kept in touch ever since. Simpson was an old-style size ten, and straight as a beam of light. He was a rare one.

"Jimmy said that?"

"Yep, you can ring 'im if you like."

That was bullshit; Jim knew nothing about it.

"Oh well, a friend of Jim's."

He pushed his glasses down and went through the Rolodex till he found the card.

"Baxter . . . is Able Seaman Otis Lewis Baxter of the SS *John P. Dean*, who is AWOL from said vessel, which docked a few weeks ago. He is believed to be over this side of the river and being assisted to remain at large by some Negro troops with whom he has some affinity unknown to me. Or so I'm informed by the Yank MPs. Now, I've told you enough. Piss off."

"Fair enough. We must have a cup of tea some day."

"Only if I've got ya locked up. Now go away, and tell Jim Simpson he keeps bad company."

He walked down to Old Cleveland Road, turned left, and sauntered along towards Stone's Corner. As he crossed over in front of the Alhambra Theatre, a big Vauxhall pulled up, coming from town. The back door opened and a voice boomed.

"Get in, Munro!"

That was quick: the Irishman must have been dialling before Jack got out the door.

It was Inspector Darkwell. A seat-polisher who'd got a long way by arselicking. Career men, they called people like him. Jack and he'd had dealings, and didn't get on.

Jack turned and jerked a thumb at the movie poster in the glass case next to him as he walked over and sat in the back of the car.

"Gee, *Mrs Miniver* was good. You oughta take the missus to see it."

"Cut the bullshit. What's your game, you nosy bastard?"

"What do you mean?"

"You know very well. You're asking questions about American matters and generally sticking your nose where it's not wanted."

"Not wanted by who?"

"By whom."

"Fuck your grammar lesson, I don't answer to you. I got fired, remember?"

"Yes, and you'd be in jail to this day if I had my way."

"Well, your bigshot cobbers decided against it as I recall, so tough titty."

The patrician figure leaned back into the leather till it squeaked.

"What's the death of the odd nigger to you, anyway? You're just a paid peeping Tom, aren't you? Don't get out of your depth."

"I just wonder about people being shot in cold blood, that's all. I mean, aren't we fighting against that sort of thing?"

"My dear chap, how the Yanks handle their nightfighters is no more our concern than it is theirs what we do with ours, for god's sake. You must have shot the occasional boong up there in the back country."

"Well no, I didn't. I chased a few over hill and dale if they'd speared some other bugger over his gin or something, but I never shot anybody, except when I was in the trenches, of course. Unlike you, I believe. Didn't you have some cushy number well away from the whizzbangs?"

"I won't take that bait, Munro. That was the *last* war, remember? I'll tell you once and for all: mind your own fucking business, and stop worrying about dead niggers and missing sailors, unless you want more trouble than you've ever seen."

"What do you know about trouble, you fucken pansy. I've had better men than you on the end of me bayonet. You don't scare me."

"There you go again." The older man sighed, then tapped the driver on the shoulder. "Take me home."

As Jack opened the door, the older man grabbed his sleeve

and looked at him coldly.

"You've been warned. Now, can I drop you somewhere?"

"I'll walk. That way I'll stay in the fresh air."

The Inspector chuckled and pointed his finger straight at him.

"Breathe it while you still can."

6

There was a slight pong from the chookshit on his trouser leg; he sloshed it about in the puddles that were forming as the rain finally started pelting down. He'd missed the last tram into town, so he had his thumb out as he stood under the Buranda Bridge. He'd slipped a row of coppers into the phone outside the railway station, and Mrs Flowers was still up. She seemed keen to hear his report in person. He could have told her what little he was going to over the phone, but he needed a bit of dosh and there might be a top-up of decent grog at the hotel.

Some provosts in a jeep picked him up after about ten minutes and he was soon strolling down Elizabeth Street.

The odd doorway held a couple going a kneetrembler, and there were a few bods still outside the Riverview Club on the Edward Street corner, but generally it was pretty quiet: nothin' like a good downpour to clean the streets of rubbish and trouble.

The private hotel lay down towards the river near the Customs House, and her room had a nice view. The johnny at the desk didn't seem at all perturbed about a bedraggled-looking bloke calling on a married woman after midnight, but what the hell, these swish buggers had their own rules.

"Take off your coat and hat," she said, after she shut the door.

He looked around; it was pretty plush, the sort of bedroom Fred and Ginger might swan about in. The long Oriental robe Mrs Flowers was wearing added to the picture.

"Can I get you a drink?"

"Sounds alright. Got any scotch? I lost mine earlier on."

"Single malt?"

"Well wacko, you do get the good stuff."

"Of course I do. Can we get down to business?"

He gave her a heavily censored version of his doings in the last twelve hours, but she still seemed impressed.

"You do get around, Mr Munro. A regular bloodhound."

He sat back pleased with himself, until she spoke again.

"But I notice you are slightly reticent on matters of detail, and you haven't really told me of any actual results from your investigation. I'm not some shrinking violet, so tell me what you really know."

This was going to be tricky.

"Can I ask how long you have been separated?"

"What sort of question is that?"

"Well, it'll help me decide how to approach this."

She stood up. "Just get on with it. What do you know?"

"Well it's just that . . . "

"I'm not afraid of bad news, Mr Munro, so tell me your worst."

"Well all I can say is . . . that he *is* definitely missing."

"Really? I know that. I'm paying you to tell me why."

"Look, I've been told that harm may well have come to him, and . . ."

"So he's dead."

"It sort of looks that way."

She didn't miss a beat.

"Do you know how?"

"I don't know how. I've only half an idea why, and no idea who . . . if he is, in fact, dead."

"Can you find out any of these things?"

"Several people have advised me not to."

"What sort of people?"

"Well . . . everybody, actually."

"That's no surprise; he wasn't a very nice man."

"Why did you marry him?"

"That's none of your concern."

Blind Freddy could see she didn't give a stuff about this clown, dead or alive. There were other reasons for tracking him down, and it wouldn't be a surprise if it was to do with money.

"Alright . . . did you love him?"

"No. Why do you ask?"

You never know till you have a go.

"So the grieving widow wouldn't need comforting then."

The whole evening had just turned on its head. A glacial pause hung in the air.

"Are you trying it on with me, Mr Munro?"

"Well . . . Yeah, actually."

More icy silence. She took a long sip of her drink, sat up straight, and ran her fingers through her hair, pushing her fringe back.

"It's raining, I'm lonely, and I suppose you'll have to do, in the absence of any other offers."

That pinned his ears back. This was some woman.

He stood up as she put her drink down and leaned back on the settee.

"But before you come anywhere near me, take off those disgusting clothes you've obviously been brawling or crawling in, and go and have a shower. I'll send them down to be cleaned."

He did as he was told, stunned by the quick turn of events.

The shower was as hot as hell. It had heaps of pressure from the boilers downstairs, and he lathered up with all the poofy unguents lying about. There was even a couple of spanking new nylon toothbrushes, so he dipped one into the tooth powder and polished up the fangs.

As he came out of the room all spruced up, she walked towards him with her robe open to the waist, her generous breasts swinging behind the silk. He started to bar up under the towel as she stood in front of him.

"Like what you see?"

"You bet," he said, wondering what to do next. This piece had it all over him.

She wrapped her arms around his neck and ground her pelvis against him. The gown fell open. She still had suspenders and stockings on, but her knickers were well away.

"Bloody hell, Mrs Flowers," he panted. "You're definitely something."

"I've got high hopes for you too, Mr Munro," she said, licking his ear.

"Call me Jack."

"Very well, Jack," she breathed. "Do whatever you want, just don't kiss me."

"What?"

"You heard. Take me as you please, but don't stick your tongue in."

He pulled her head back by her long blonde tresses and looked into her eyes.

"How about I kiss you somewhere else then."

She paused as if weighing it up.

"I'd like to try that . . ."

Another pause hung in the air.

"Do what you want, just remember the rules."

The storm had cleared and a cool breeze parted the curtains as they grappled with each other on the huge bed.

He felt the soft slide of the silk stockings against his ears.

No rule that couldn't be broken some way or other.

7

SATURDAY

He was still a long way from the finish line when the phone rang, and it was a welcome respite. He rolled off as she leant over to answer it, and lay back puffing: backing up for a morning glory was still a fair enough call at his age, but this was taking so long he was beginning to wonder if there was any shot left in the locker. Mrs Flowers (or Julia, as he had found out during the night) wasn't complaining, but the prospect of picking it up later was very appealing.

It was the concierge, inquiring as to the breakfast arrangements, and he took the opportunity to head for the shower, while proclaiming that whatever came up had better be hearty, as he hadn't had a decent feed since Thursday night.

As they sat down to the full English at the tiny table, he felt he'd known her for years. He started fantasising about keeping a good thing going, and all that happily ever after stuff.

She broke the spell with one statement.

"So how much do I pay you for your services, Jack?'

The familiarity was just a thin veneer on an icy reserve that had grown stronger with the intensity of the sunlight that crept across the floor. She might be a tiger under the sheets in the wee small hours, but it was business as usual in the hard light of day.

"Well, it's usually ten quid a day plus expenses, but it evens out over few weeks if I'm required for that long."

She produced a wad of lobsters and counted out 10 of them.

"Here's a deposit then."

"It's usually me who pays for a night like that!" he joked, and immediately tried to pull the words back in.

Too late. It went down badly, and she turned away. He looked for his wallet.

"It's in the drawer along with your firearm," she said. "I couldn't very well leave it there for the staff to see."

As if on cue, there was another knock at the door and she took delivery of his suit and shoes. Everything was spick and span, except for the fact that he had no clean underwear. This getting dressed and leaving stuff was even harder to do in a dignified manner than getting the kit off in the first place, and it made him aware that he was becoming superfluous to proceedings. His place was back out on the snoop, and they both knew it.

"I've got a few clothes at the office," he said.

"Very well," she said, "you'd best pop along then."

"I'll call you."

"Of course."

He went to kiss her goodbye, but she pulled back.

"Like a bloody pro," he thought.

As he went out the door she suddenly grabbed his arm and whispered, "Be careful."

He winked, put on his hat, and headed for the stairs. All was not lost.

They reckon you shouldn't give 'em all you've got on the first night, so they don't get disappointed next time round, but he didn't subscribe to that. A piece like her doesn't come along every day, so you go for broke. He hadn't let the side down, that's for sure.

The streets of the city had that sparkling feel as the shopkeepers hosed down whatever the rain hadn't washed off the footpaths, and the sun had yet to penetrate right down to street level. The newsstands were quieter than on a weekday, and the smell of baking bread wafted around. He decided a nice walk back to the office while the day was young wouldn't be a bad idea, and he sauntered up Queen Street, past Allan & Stark's, whistling and thinking: Give us ya worst, ya bastards. I'm up for it.

He would get his wish.

He noticed a US staff car parked down a side street near the Trocadero as he came along Melbourne Street from the Vic Bridge: a Yank officer dropping some bint off after a big night in the backseat, no doubt. Good luck to him; he can't have done better than the old Mower.

Leo was putting boxes of fruit out. Jack cheekily swiped an apple as he greeted the family and took off up the stairs.

He'd just dropped his strides to put on a clean pair of ball-catchers when three khaki figures loomed the other side of the frosted glass door.

He shouted out, "Give us a tick!"

But they just barged in. He was still doing up his fly when they reached his desk.

"I told ya these Ossies are always playin' with 'emselves, didn't I, Frank?" said the taller of the two MPs. They were the hard nuts from the night before, and they looked like even bigger bastards in the cold light of day.

They accompanied an officer with more braid hanging off him than the foyer of a flash cinema. He had the rock jaw, too-clear blue eyes, and big teeth of some Hollywood pretty boy, and carried himself with the easy arrogance of the well-connected and nasty. Aviator glasses completed the picture of a man who had obviously studied MacArthur very closely.

"Hey, that's not very Allied of ya, Chuck," said the blue-eyed one. "We're all here to combat the enemy's plans for world domination."

Jack laughed.

"Chuck, eh? Hah! I like that!"

"Whadya mean, asshole?" he said, leaning forward with his nightstick half out of the ring on his belt.

"Well, 'chuck' has a different meaning in this country."

"Is that so?"

"Yeah, it's something usually found in the shithouse or the gutter. So I think it applies quite well in this case."

That riled him.

"You jackshit malingerer!"

"Hold it!" yelled the officer. "Let's get onto a more friendly basis here. I'm Lieutenant-Colonel Tremayne, US Army, and these are my personal assistants."

Jack stood there bemused. The bloody Yanks handed out commissions like dog licenses. This bastard couldn't have been more than thirty years old, and he already outranked men who had probably given years of active service . . . what a fucken war.

"Nice to meet you. And how can I help you this sunny morning?"

Tremayne played with a pencil he'd picked up off Jack's desk.

"I have been informed that you are involving yourself in matters that come under the purview of the US Army's enforcement of military discipline."

"Meaning?"

"Fraternisation in areas reserved for the recreation of coloured troops."

"It's a free country, ya know."

"Your own government has expressed concern at the highest level about the deleterious effect of the Nigra troops on the morale of the population."

"Not to me."

Tremayne tapped the pencil on the desk, then put it down carefully.

"Very droll, but I can assure you that I am concerned about your activities constituting an impediment to the war effort."

Jack had heard enough.

"What a lotta hot shit! You're not making much fucking effort that I can see! Ever been in a foxhole, Major-General, or whatever you are? You're a bloody marshmallow. What's all that fruit salad for? Conspicuous gallantry in seat-warming?"

The smaller MP leaned forward, like Joe E. Brown without the smile.

"Yew got a bad mouth, mister. Now yew show some respect to the Colonel here, or I'll whup you bad."

"Would that be by yourself, or with some assistance from your gorilla mate over 'ere?"

Tremayne interjected, and he'd lost his fake politeness.

"Goddamn you, feller! We come over here to save your busted-ass country, and where's the gratitude, huh? First sign of trouble, your pissant army folds up along with those worthless limey faggots, and now we gotta come in and rescue this fucked-up backwater so you can keep livin' like white folks! So wise up. We're here to stay and we're doing it our way – so get *out* of the way! Got it?"

Jack couldn't stifle a chuckle.

"You mean like Dugout Doug got out of the way at Corregidor?"

That was blasphemy to the gilded one. He turned to his two

pals and shouted, "If you see this bastard anywhere near *anybody* in a US uniform, nigger, white, or brindle, you kick his ass and throw him in the guardhouse! And we'll keep him there till the end of the war, if he lives that long. Let's go!"

Chuck turned as they left.

"I got your number, wise-ass."

"I didn't think ya could count, ya palooka!"

As soon as they were gone, he sat down. There was more to this than he thought: they were just too sensitive.

What was one little spiv running round flogging a few army goodies? And yet the whole town was warning Jack off – and Reg Flowers himself had no doubt been knocked on the head.

A sensible feller would mooch around pretending to check it all out, jump back in the sack with the wife if that was still on offer, and spend the dough wisely. He wasn't that man.

He opened the cupboard and took out his police-issue hobnails: there'd be no soft-shoe shuffling from here on. Beside them was a nice pearl-handled flick-knife that fitted into a little ankle holster; he put that on as well.

It was gunna be a long day.

8

The phone rang and rang until a gruff voice answered.

"Do you know what time it is?"

"Time you were up, boofhead."

"Fuck, Jack, it's the crack of dawn!"

"It's about eleven, ya bludger. We have to talk."

"Mate, leave us alone, will ya? I had a big one."

"Let me guess, the raffle went your way?"

"No mate, I'm not that silly. The brothers don't like to see snouts in the trough. Those most accommodating young sheilas all went to thoroughly deserving and fully paid-up members."

"Fuck, you could talk that union guff under twenty foot of wet cement."

"Anyway, whattya want."

"I need to talk."

"Aw, what about? Not that missing nonce again, is it?"

"Not on the phone."

"This is pushing the friendship, sport."

"Do us the favour, will ya? Stroll down to the Norman Park ferry and I'll meet ya on your side."

"You're using up ya points with this, mate . . . Give me an hour."

He sat in the rear driver's compartment with his feet up on the handle-post and watched the street unrolling behind the tram as it headed out past the Gabba railway yards. By now, there was no way anyone could have followed him. No car could have been slow enough to have remained in the traffic behind them, and none had appeared again after waiting up. Unless they had a whole fleet shadowing him, he was alright.

The river reflected clouds as the tram crossed the Norman Creek Bridge. There was no wind, and the water was like glass. He got off at the stop halfway up Galloways Hill and strolled down through the little park to the river. The ferry was on the other side, so he sat listening to the lapping sound of the water on the piles. It was peaceful, and timeless.

He was the only passenger on the little timber ferry. He sat at the back as it burbled its way over the opposite side, where he saw Lenny throwing a cigarette butt into the water.

He alighted, and they walked into New Farm Park in silence, until they were well away from the families and couples spread out on the grass.

"Right, what's this all about."

"The SS *John P. Dean*."

"What about it?"

"There's some Yanks real upset with me, and I think it's because I've touched a nerve. But I dunno what it is. The same blokes putting the standover on me are also lookin' for some prick off this ship, so I wanna know why it's all so important."

"Mate, you're heading into dangerous waters."

"So."

The union man stood back, his thumbs in his vest pockets, and stared up at the sky, then at the ground, before speaking.

"Look, this ship docked about five or six weeks back, alright?

It comes in just before knock-off, so we tick it down for tomorrow's unloading."

"Of what?"

"All sorts of shit. Mostly stuff like uniforms, a few crates of jeeps and bikes, one hold fulla medicines."

"Really, what sort?"

"O you know. Fucken bandages and pills and bottles of this and that. I dunno. It didn't go into that much detail on the manifest."

"So what about it."

"Well the funny thing was, the whole crew took immediate shore leave, just all shot through, virtually as soon as they tied up."

"Is that unusual? It's a long haul."

"Yeah, but there's usually a few old salts and married men rostered on to keep everything ticking over, you know; pumps and power and stuff. This one they seem to have all fucked off quick smart."

"And?"

"So anyway, Bob Prendergast is working late in his office, and he can see down the dock to where this thing's tied up. He sees this figure shoot out from behind all these piles of dunnage, clamber up the gangway and head for the front hold – and not towards the crew's end.

"Now Bob's a sly old bugger, and can see this isn't quite right, so he trots over and up on board to see if he can work out what this joker's up to. He goes down into the hold and can't see nothin', but then he sees a hatch open goin' further down, so he shins down there . . . and next thing he can hear this rushing sound from below. Bugger me if it isn't one of the seacocks – some bastard's trying to scuttle the bloody thing! It's not too far gone for Bob to get in there up to his armpits and turn it off, but next thing this other joker flies up the ladder and away. Bob's still pretty quick, so he's chased him up through the hold, up the fucken ladders and onto the deck, and tackled the bastard."

"Ya can't keep an old League player down . . . Brothers, wasn't it?"

"Yeah, and Wests. Anyway, there's a bit of a struggle, and next thing the bastard's over the side and into the drink. It's a bloody long drop, so Bob races down onto the dock to see if the bloke's floating, but no go. So he rouses the shore patrol, and the bastards tell him he's dreamin'. 'Am I?' says Bob, 'well how about this fucken hat then?' He's got hold of the bloke's rag hat, and there's the name inside."

"Baxter."

"Yeah . . . how'd you know?"

"That's why we're talking, mate."

"Anyway, there was a bit of a kerfuffle, and hemming and hahing, and that was that."

"So what happened then?"

"Well, the funny thing was, the next day, first thing, a whole regiment's worth of trucks turn up, and we have to load all the medicine out of that hold, and straight off the docks it goes.

No sorting out, no nothin'. It was all going straight to Greenslopes Hospital, according to the paperwork. Some big-shot was there, ordering every prick around, and it was all gone as soon as we could get it on the wharf."

"That wouldn't have been a real flash bastard by the name of Tremayne, would it?"

"Mate, I couldn't say, But he *was* a bit of a glamorous lookin' prick, sunglasses an' all.

"Gotta be him."

"Your turn, Jack. What's happening?"

"I think Reggie swiped some stuff from these fellas, which

never got near no bloody hospital, for obvious shonky reasons, and they got upset. Which is why they didn't just hand him over to the local plods. But you don't go knockin' off some joker over a bit of the five-finger discount; there's gotta be more to it."

"Watch yourself, mate. I told ya before, this is poison."

Jack looked searchingly at his old comrade.

"You're tellin' me everything, aren't ya, mate? Ya wouldn't leave me hangin'."

Lenny was insulted.

"Mate, you know what I know, alright?"

Jack had to take him at his word. That's what mates are for.

"Good enough for me."

They parted, and he headed back to the ferry. The river had begun to roll with the change of tide, like the force that was drawing him further and further into this dark puzzle. But, that was always the way of it: in till the end, for better or worse.

9

The answer had to lie at the depot in Coorparoo. He was in the area, and it would put some more pieces in place if he could get confirmation. There was a small shop on the corner of Norman Avenue, so he stopped in and bought a corned beef sandwich from the old dear behind the counter. He took her up on her offer of a cup of tea and drank it black, like the old days. They discussed the war and the weather before he got directions and set off at a leisurely pace towards the Norman Park station. He had a long wait there too. The bushflies pestered him as he paced the platform, kicking gravel onto the rails to see if he could make them ring. The train pulled in, and he went one stop, then got off and handed his ticket to the young lad at the foot of the stairs.

"Where's the Yank warehouse round here, sport?" he enquired. The spotty boy pushed the too-large cap back off his pasty forehead at a rakish angle and said, "Just down there to the left, digga."

He winked and clucked his tongue, then went up the stairs over the level crossing and down Cavendish Road towards the creek. It was as deserted as any industrial area is on a weekend, and he'd stick out like dog's balls on the street, so he pushed a bit of old cyclone wire aside on a vacant block and headed through it towards the railway embankment that ran behind the buildings. There was a goat-track at the bottom, covered in rubbish; he hoped it would give him some cover as he figured out the lie of the land. After a hundred yards or so he came to an area with a long line of pallets stacked about twenty foot high right along the back fence, and a Negro soldier sitting on a drum having a smoke. He crept up to the corner of the fence and rattled the wire.

The sergeant looked around, startled. "What you doin' there? Hey, you that guy from the cathouse las' night."

"That's me," he replied. "Look, I know you aren't supposed to give this kind of information, but . . ."

"Damn right. Get the hell away from here."

"Half a mo'. . . Is this warehouse full of stuff from the *Dean*?"

"How'd you know that?"

"Well I didn't, but I do now."

"Shit man, you really askin' for trouble. Beat it. I ain't said nothin'. Those muthafuckas would kill me, man, like a bug!"

"Exactly. Which is why I need to know what's going on if I'm to help."

"Man, just get yo' ass away from here. I ain't never seen ya. Those assholes be watchin' this place real close. I can't even trust all my own boys. You get seen here, we both in big trouble. I'm gone. Don't *never* come near me again."

With that the sergeant stubbed out his cigarette and fairly bolted over to the back door of the old timber building, then slammed it shut behind him.

Jack squatted on his heels and thought for a minute. These clowns had definitely put the fear into everyone associated with whatever was going on. Time to see if they were as bad as their word. He scrambled up the embankment and started heading along the main line towards town.

As he strolled along the track the sun began to sink low. He was no stranger to the rails; he'd always played on them where the main western line crossed his parent's property on the Downs. There weren't many other kids about, so he hung around the tracks on weekends to wave at passengers who went past.

Sometimes he went down to the bridge across the gully when the mail train went through at night. He climbed under the span so he was close under the track, and the roaring machine thundered right over him, belching steam. It was a test of nerve, and he later took it to the extreme of sitting at the level of the track with his head resting on the sleeper, his nose only inches from the junction of wheel and rail, while a speeding locomotive hurtled through. The adrenaline rush and cacophony were incredible, and he could have been killed, but he did it anyway. The remorseless will and discipline that was forged on those nights stood him in good stead years later under barrage on the Western Front: when other blokes flipped and started sobbing or screaming, he'd just sit in his dugout, seeing those flashing steel wheels at the edge of his nose, and ride it out.

Jack got to the bridge over Norman Creek and clambered down the slope to the edge of the slimy green pool at the bottom of the stanchions. There was no-one around the footbridge over the creek to Deshon Street. There was a large dirt turning circle underneath the bridge, and the whole area was surrounded by reeds that grew in huge thickets from the banks of the creek. It was a lonely spot, no doubt perfect for a bit of nookie after dark for the locals, but quiet and desolate in the late afternoon heat.

He squatted on his heels and looked at the ground closely from a different angle relative to the sun. You could spot some tracks better that way. He was no expert, but he'd picked up a few pointers from King Billy, the tracker who went out with him to bring in Myalls while Jack was exiled at the remote outpost in the spinifex following his efforts during the strike. His real name was Baccy Billy Murri, but he was a king among trackers as far as Jack was concerned, so that's what he called him, to Billy's constant embarrassment.

"I'm no king, boss," he'd say, "just an ordinary feller."

That he wasn't. He could look at some gibbers and point out where a kangaroo had farted a week previous. He could sense water an hour's walk away and tell how long a dry leaf had been on the ground. Jack reckoned he could track a moth through a sandstorm.

They shared many a campfire yarn, and Jack asked him once how he felt about tracking down his own people. He laughed and said: "I only track a feller from some other mob. We'd only be fighting over things in the old days anyway. If he's my mob . . . I lose him."

It was Billy who'd helped him find a downed plane and save the dying son of a wealthy businessman, which had earned Jack his ticket back to the smoke. He missed the old bugger and hoped he was still at large in some remote spot, hadn't drifted into any of the towns. He needed him now.

Jack walked down a bit further, and saw unmistakable jeep tracks in the soft earth. He got down closer, and sure enough: a couple of cartridge cases, then further over, a dark mass covered in ants. Some bad business had indeed been done down here. He was so absorbed that he didn't hear the footfalls behind him until it was too late, until the unmistakable click of a weapon being cocked made him jump up and turn around.

They had him cold. The slimy one called Frank had a Thompson pointed square at his guts, and his good mate Chuck had his billy club out and was gently rubbing up and down it like it was his dick.

This was no good . . . . he was too old, too slow, and now he was gunna cop it. But there was no way he was going down like a cur, so he opened up with some lip.

"Down here for a quick bit of lovin' are ya, fellers? All them hours in the jeep holdin' hands."

Chuck laughed.

"Your cobber digger smartass mouth won't save ya this time. Put your goddamn hands up."

He searched round his belt and came up with the Colt.

"Well now, what have we here, Franklin? This looks like a US-issue weapon, stolen by this fifth columnist to be treacherously used against our forces. You can get jail for this, boy."

"Fuck off, I've seen your mob swap one for a bottle. And that one was left behind with a sheila 'cause the clown had no dough."

"You implyin' a lack of patriotism and moral fibre in our troops? I won't stand for that."

He swung the club like a baseball bat and got Jack right below the hip. He went down like a knocked horse. This was quickly followed by a flurry of boots, and Jack quickly got into a foetal position, one arm behind his back to protect his kidneys, and stuck it out. They knew their stuff: the billy club pummeled his back and the boots sank into his ribs, but they stayed away from his head. They weren't out to kill him, but he was gunna be fucken sore.

After a couple of minutes he was a shot duck. He lay there gasping, in more pain than he could ever remember. A couple of ribs had crunched, but they'd not gone with a clean break, would only be splintered at worst, and he wouldn't have to worry about puncturing anything when he got up. Which would be a while yet.

Chuck leant down, stuck the barrel of the .45 in Jack's mouth and snarled:

"Now listen here, you nosy bastard, hear this good. If I ever see you again, I'm gonna shove this up your no-good kangaroo ass and pull the fucken trigger, and believe me, you will die very slowly. You got me?"

"Clear as mud, sport," he grunted.

Chuck stood up and gave Jack one more kick just as a couple of kids with fishing rods appeared. As they stared wide-eyed at the scene, Chuck walked over to them.

"Hiya kids. Wanna chocolate bar?"

"Yes please, mister!"

He handed out some goodies as Jack lay there in the dust.

"Is he a bad man, mister?"

"Sure is. This fella's no good, kids. But we fixed him, and that's what happens when ya stand in the way of the USA."

"Do you know John Wayne?" offered one of the tykes through a gobful of toffee.

"He's my close personal buddy," Chuck snorted, then walked back to Jack and said quietly, "You're a lucky feller. You'd be soaking in our piss right now if these little guys hadn't turned up. Then louder, "Take care now. Time to go."

The two MPs strolled off sniggering, back around the embankment towards the warehouse.

Jack sat up gingerly. The bastards must have spotted him back there. He hoped it was after he saw the sergeant, or else worse might happen to him. He dusted himself off and looked at the kids. What did they know? It was all a movie to them, war and all.

Jack knew he was in bad shape, but it would be worse if he lay down again now. Wherever that was would be where he would stay for at least a couple of days. He'd gone off a nag once and ended up lying in a shed, pissing in a tin for a week. No, he had to see this out on his feet, whatever happened.

It was pretty clear what was going on: these bastards were running a racket, and weren't keen on sharing the action. The scale of the operation was no surprise really; the Yanks went over the top in everything. All he had to do was find this Reg prick and then hand the whole show over to the cops – if he could find one who wasn't in on it. At least Jimmy Simpson was straight; Jack would have to clue him in and leave it up to them. This was getting too rough.

He started walking up Deshon Street, but only got as far as the phone booth outside the shop on the corner of Railway Street before he bunged in the pennies and called a cab. He was getting too old for this caper. Following philanderers round was a lot easier. He sat in the gutter and waited, breathing heavily. The sound of boys playing out a game of cricket echoed in the distance. It was hot.

10

Eye contact between men is a complicated business, and it can be useful to know its rules and irregularities.

You can't hold a bloke's gaze for too long on first meeting: it invites aggression through invasion of imagined personal space, or he might think you're a horse's. By the same token, if you can't meet his gaze for any length of time, it makes you seem suspicious . . . It's a fine art, so Jack knew that the fella over by the bar in the brown suit wasn't there for fun. For one thing he was dawdling over a pony; he also looked away far too quick when he cased Jack coming in. A normal feller going about his business will give ya the once over without a squirm, but not this joker. Either he was a fizgig, or he was there to tip off someone about Jack's movements – Soupy, presumably. Jack worked his way around the side of the bar so he wouldn't have to push through the crowd with his tender ribs. The fact that there *was* still beer available meant that the crowd wouldn't thin out until closing; some blokes were anticipating that dreadful moment and had rows of foaming pots lined up in front of them. Jack didn't get a chance to order one before the brown suit suddenly drained his glass and took off, avoiding his gaze.

That was enough. Jack went to the window and watched as

the figure headed away from the pub at a fast clip, looking over his shoulder. As soon as the brown suit went round the corner, Jack stepped out the side door and followed him. He wasn't going back to the Majestic, he was heading down to the river; he turned onto the wharves at Glenelg Street then headed south towards the dry dock.

Jack kept a safe distance, but the man wasn't looking behind him now as he hurried towards a peeling timber door next to a loading bay and went inside. Jack crept up to the door and saw that it had been left ajar. He could hear no sound, so he pushed it slightly open, and looked inside. There was an office up a flight of stairs to the left. He could hear people talking in there, but the angle of vision prevented them from having a view of the door. Opposite was the wide entrance to a cold store, from which rubber strips hung to the floor, letting small lines of light out across the wet concrete. Jack darted across and slid through the strips into the cold room. It was a chilled holding area; thick doors led off the passageway to the actual freezers. The rail system was loaded with more beef than he'd seen in a while. That Soupy didn't miss a trick.

Shortages meant that any slaughtered meat the army didn't get went straight to the butcher quick smart, and wasn't hung for any length of time. This so-called "hot" meat was usually as tough as an old boot. Most people had to subsist on mutton anyway, so no bugger had sat down to a decent tender steak for ages. This beef would be worth a packet at the back door of the toffs' hangouts and officer's clubs; the rows of carcasses added up to a sizeable investment – and a bigger return. A lot of palms would've been greased to keep this operation going. No wonder the fat man didn't want any fuss about a few crook bandages to spoil his day. Jack wandered further into the labyrinth of beef. There was row upon row of it, and when he opened the doors to the freezers he saw even more lined up. He went into the last room and stopped short. The figure seated on the office chair looked quite relaxed, until you realised that he was tied to it, and frozen stiff.

The pencil moustache was outlined in white where his last breaths had solidified, and the eyes were closed. It was Reg, the missing spiv, and he'd just gone to sleep in his shirtsleeves, by the look of things.

The dim light and clouds of steam from his own breath gave the whole scene a solemn air as Jack looked carefully at the floor.

There were footprints everywhere in the thin muddy slush that covered it, as well as lots of continuous lines. It was easy to work out. The chair had left tracks, showing he'd been wheeled in and out. A simple form of torture when you think about it: leave him in there until he's nearly dead, then wheel him out again to thaw out. Not the right answer, fella? Back in ya go, and so on . . . until he either told them what they wanted to know, or gave up the ghost. The bastards probably left him in there either way.

Jack tiptoed back to the main entrance and peered sideways through the rubber strips.

His blood ran colder than it was already. Those bloody MPs were there in the office, and they were looking down at the doorway.

Jesus, these bastards were everywhere. If they came in, he'd be in the icebox with Reg, and it'd be all over red rover. Half-ruptured, no gun, and four blokes to take on . . . this was grim.

He could hope they'd piss off, or he could hide amongst the beef, but that could go badly wrong if they locked him in. Shit. Curiosity might freeze the fucken cat if he wasn't careful. He looked around. The rail that carried the hooks had a junction to either send it round the corner to another room or connect to the dock rail outside once the door was opened. He grabbed the wire and disconnected the turn-off, and then went down the outside rail and connected up a branch so that he could select a run. He had to push the carcasses very slowly so as not to make any noise when the wheels ran over the junctions, but the fan's background hum would mask most of it. He soon had five quarters lined up, and a full side at the back to protect him down to knee level.

A quick check again showed that he had been on the money. They were coming down the stairs. The cockatoo headed for the street, which improved the odds a bit, but it would still be tricky. Jack made a quick estimation of how long it would take the rest of them to get the cold room entrance, then got behind the full side about a dozen yards back. The voices got closer, and then he saw a hand part the strips.

He pushed as hard as he could, ignoring the pain, and got the beef rolling. By the time he got up to running speed, the first MP and Soupy were brushing the strips aside, and they looked up in amazement as a row of carcasses hurtled towards them, swinging from side to side. The surprise was complete: they had no time to react as the best part of a ton of meat shot off the end of the rail, bowled them out of the way and tumbled over them, flattening the MP bringing up the rear. Jack raced out through the rubber and kept going, straight over the pile of tangled men and forequarters on the floor. As he shot past, he could see that the combined weight of Soupy Jones and the travelling beef had completely ironed out one MP, and, as the hook and roller came off, one piece had caught the fat one in the eye and laid him out like a dead man. The second MP was dazed and trying to get out from under all the meat, but Jack was across the loading area and out onto the dock in a flash. He headed down towards the

Fish Market, but he'd only got about fifty yards when a small piece of the timber dock flew up, followed by a sharp crack: the Yanks had regained themselves and were bolting down the wharf after him, letting off rounds all over the place.

"Fucken lunatics," he grunted, and ran towards where a trawler was being unloaded. They couldn't fire now, and he swerved in and out of the aproned men and their barrows piled high with mullet and bream, then raced into the main building.

There was no point going out onto the street, so he hunched over and crept around the columns and benches until he found himself up at the Victoria Bridge end. He could hear the Yanks cursing and rampaging around inside the market, so he kept low and headed back to the edge of the dock, where service steps led down underneath the wharf.

He went down, then clambered back along the struts between the piles and made it to the shore. The tide was low, so he could actually walk on the stony bank in the gloom and not get wet. He stood behind a piling with his knife out. Hand-to-hand it would have to be, if he could get close enough. He waited in the darkness.

They didn't come; he'd slipped the net again. He could hear lots of swearing above him, muffled by the timbers, but couldn't risk going back up to check it out.

After about an hour, he headed slowly along the edge of the water that sloshed around the piles, and gradually worked his way towards the Burke's Wharf end of Stanley Street. There'd be some access up there somewhere, and he could work out what to do on the way.

11

The pain was really starting to bite. As Jack surfaced at street level, he realised he wasn't too far from Doctor Dix's. That wasn't the doc's real name: it was Trebilcock, and he had once reigned in his fancy rooms up on the Terrace as a gyno to the high and mighty, who sent their wives and daughters to him in the strictest confidence that any unforeseen problems could be dealt with discreetly. It was rumoured that he was also under contract to the Catholic Church to deal with any unwanted consequences of capers in the convent. Legend even had it that a lime-filled mass grave of clerical by-blows was to be found behind the walls of a New Farm nunnery, or so the Prods would darkly claim. His fall from grace had been precipitated by his inability to keep his internal probings strictly professional; eventually a relief nurse caught him up to his nuts in the 14-year old daughter of a government minister. The hearings to have him struck off were held in camera, so as to protect all the guilty, but the axe still fell. Dix now resided in a dingy house in Merivale Street and survived by scraping out the wombs of the careless in the district, as well as patching up the odd knife or bullet wound that wouldn't stand scrutiny up at the Mater. A blind eye was probably turned because at least he knew what he was doing. His patients always survived, unlike an increasing number of young girls messed up by backyard butchers in the rush to remove the social stain of over-eager fraternisation with the smiling invaders.

Dix's name wasn't a nom-de-plume: it had come about due to the unwillingness (or inability) of the demimonde to pronounce his name correctly, as Tra-bilco; they, of course, called him Treble-cock – and, by extension, Three Dicks.

He wasn't a bad man, just bitter and unpleasant; Jack didn't take much of a shine to him, but if anyone could sort him out with some painkillers on the sly, then Dr Dix it was.

There weren't many lights in the street but Jack still didn't muck about; he cracked on at a fair pace until he was at the front steps of Dix's house. Broken louvres dangled each side of the door, and the usual smell of cat piss was swamped by the pungent reek of ether. Jack hoped the doc wasn't in the middle of some cut-rate carving, but he had to get off the street in a hurry, so he shot around the back and up the rear stairs. Dr Dix sat in the kitchen in a dressing-gown, unshaven and holding a footy sock to his nose while cackling like a madman. The smell of ether was intense, and Jack realised the doc was off his trolley on the stuff, and had been for a while. He sat down.

"Ya there, are ya, Doc?"

The glazed eyes came into focus.

"Fuck me backwards, old chap. How are you?"

"Not good, mate. What's this caper?"

"Just a brief slosh of Mother E, old boy. Nothing to get in a lather about."

"What are ya doin' with that shit? Isn't it supposed to knock you out?"

"Not mixed with the right amount of oxygen, it won't. In fact you have the most *wonderful* time, you know."

"Really? I'll stick to the neck oil, thanks. That stuff stinks."

"My dear boy, it's quicker and cheaper than that, and the visions are just fabulous. But anyway, what's up . . . said the Doc!"

He giggled helplessly.

Jack shook his head in wonderment, then continued. "Mate, I'm in a bit of strife, and I've took a bit of a hiding. Can ya fix me up with some heavy-duty stuff?"

The doctor straightened up a bit in his chair, and seemed to come good. "Give me a look."

A brief examination ensued and then he sat back. "Nothing broken there, but you'll bruise up nicely. So what can I do?"

"Well, tape us up and give me something so I can keep goin', for a start."

"Oh my dear chap, you really should be at home in bed with that little lot."

"Well I can't. It's a bit dicey."

"Isn't it always? Say no more. The only problem is . . . I don't have any painkillers at the mo."

"What? You do all sorts of stuff here . . . what's the story?"

The doc sucked in his breath and sat back on the creaky chair.

"Terrible tale, don't you know. I bought a huge pile of stuff from that Soupy character." He sniffed. "Dreadful chap . . . not only was it all utter rubbish, but the bloody Yanks came round and took it all back – without reimbursement of any kind!"

"Hang on, what Yanks?"

"Well it was all their gear, wasn't it."

"Let me guess: Medical Corps stuff?"

"Yes indeed, bloody scads of it: bandages, saline, chloroform, morphine, the whole wack. Two hundred bloody quid's worth."

"And?"

"Well it was all no good, I tell you! The bloody morphine was just water, there was no salt in the saline, the bandages were just rags when you unwrapped them and so on. A complete shambles. I went back to Soupy to complain, and the next thing I knew these two awful gorillas appeared and confiscated the lot, with some pretty dire warnings not to tell anyone."

"So let me get this right: it looked all tickety-boo on the outside, but when you opened it up, it was all just shit an' rubbish?"

"Exactly, old boy."

"And the Yanks didn't call the local wallopers, they just loaded it up and pissed off."

"Precisely."

The Doc stretched the crepe hard, and slapped on a couple of yards of Elastoplast.

Jack put his shirt back on gingerly.

"Deary me, doc. It's a dreadful world we live in when crooks are robbin' each other . . . But anyway, back to the matter in hand: I'm half-dead, and you're the sawbones . . . do something."

The dishevelled figure's eyes brightened.

"Aha! I might have just the thing."

He got on his knees, pushed aside the mop and bucket in the small alcove by the door and came up with a small brown bottle.

"This'll do it. The bloody cat knocked it over and all the alcohol's dried up, but the base is still there."

"What's this fucken poison, mate?"

"Opium, you bloody fool. This is a laudanum bottle, and what's left in there is pure opium. Just smear a bit onto a Tally-Ho and roll it up in a durry, you'll be right as rain."

"Do I look like fucken Fu Manchu? And I don't smoke anymore."

"It'll work, my dear chap, and that's what counts. Look, here's one of my briars, that'll be even better. And because I'm just about the best bloke you'll ever meet, here's half a tin of

Havelock. Ah, the clarity of mind on the ether, old boy! It is *truly* fabulous."

"But it'll knock me out, ya stupid deaf bastard; I gotta stay a moving target."

The doc reached into his gown.

"Take two of these, and you won't sleep till the middle of the week. That'll be ten pounds, my good man."

The street light under the huge mango tree threw patterns on the ground as Jack walked carefully along the edge of Musgrave Park. He had to get back to the office to get his .38, but the whole suburb was now enemy territory. He hunched in his overcoat, sweating and trying not to moan as the footfalls jarred his ribs. He wanted to smoke the O to kill the pain, but it would slow him down too much. The sky was swollen with cloud, and lightning flared in the western sky as he cut through various alleys until he emerged near the office. He slipped through Leo's back gate, trying not to trip over crates of drink bottles, and tapped gently on the back door. Mrs Madrakis answered; he hushed her and whispered: "Is anyone up at my office?"

"Yes, some army men. They have been there for a while, Mr Jack."

Shit, that's torn it.

He sat down in the kitchen wondering what to do, when Leo came in and handed him a piece of paper. "Some black man leave this for you this afternoon."

It read, *Meet me at Doboy station, dawn. Baxter.*

Doboy was a good place to meet someone on the sly: a meat-worker's siding down near the river with no station office, it sat in the middle of some swampy scrub, pretty isolated.

"Can you give me something to eat on the run, mate?" he asked.

"Of course Mr Jack, we say nothing. Eleni, get some cheese, olives, bread."

They handed him a small flour bag with the food, and a bottle of ginger beer.

"Go careful, my friend."

Jack turned up his coat collar against the wind and drizzle that was whipping down the street, headed straight over to the station and bought a ticket for Lota. The train was sitting there waiting, and he went all the way along till he found an empty carriage, quickly grabbed the handle at the rear, then pulled it over, shutting off the lights inside. The darkness swallowed him as he slumped on the bench seat with his hat over his eyes and waited for departure.

He was safer here than just about anywhere, and he'd be first at Doboy in the morning to sniff out the lay of the land. These bloody Yanks were all over him so far, and he needed a bit of space to let the dog see the rabbit.

The stationmaster blew his whistle, and the carriage jumped, jarring his ribs. He hauled out the wax vestas. Time to have that smoke.

12

SUNDAY

It was a long night pacing the platform, with the mournful calls of the marsh birds echoing like the cries of the dead. Jack had steeled himself against stretching out on the bench; the pipe would have made it soft, and he knew he wouldn't get up again in a hurry. No, just keep walking and thinking, awake and dreaming at the same time. As he puffed on the pipe to kill the pain, everything had a certain tinge to it, and his mind was both slow and racing. As the moon rose and set, time folded in on itself.

The dawn was rainy and grey, and he sensed someone approaching before he saw him.

It was a lean figure, as furtive as a graveyard rat. He had the rawboned look of someone who'd never had a three-course meal as a kid, but could work all day on a cup of tea and a slice of bread.

"So what's the story, Baxter?"

"What do you wanna know?"

He had one of those deep south accents like Tremayne, and he was scared.

"I'm just a feller trying to get to the bottom of a few mysteries in the district. In your case, why did you try and scuttle the boat? Are you a saboteur or what?"

"It'll cost ya, buddy."

He took a few tenners out and peeled off one . . . two . . . three . . . four . . . and then another, until the little man reached out.

"I ain't no traitor. They told me to do it."

"Who told ya to?"

"The Secret Service guys, army spies, you know."

"No I don't. Back up a bit and give me the full story; the first train won't be along for hours. Let's have some brekkie."

They sat in the shelter, out of the rain.

"Want a sanger?"

"Surely."

Jack cut a slice off the hard loaf with his flick-knife as Baxter began his tale.

It was a real saga: he'd robbed a "gas station" at fifteen. His sister needed medicine. He only got twenty bucks. They caught him. He got life. The state penitentiary. Jail rape. Knife fights. The chain gang. A breakout. On the run shackled to a black man. It didn't matter who was what colour in his part of Louisiana; they were all dirt poor. Hiding in the swamps. Finally he got to New Orleans, took some ID off a drunk in an alley, and joined the Merchant Marine.

"I already done two trips out here," he said. "I went down on the *Sam Smith* a hundred mile south of Tokelau, and believe me that's a lonely place. Spent four days in the water, lost buddies to sharks, the whole goddamn box an' dice. If our radio man hadn't been still sendin' as she went down, that'd be my story over right there. I ain't no traitor, man."

"So why did you open the sea-cocks that night?"

"Well, ain't that a funny story. Last time I was back stateside, I got spotted. Some feller recognised me from prison, and we had a fight.

"I ended up in the stockade, and while I was waiting for them to find me out and send me back, these black hat dudes took me for a ride. They said, 'We know who you are. You belong to us. You do as we say or you're back on the chain-gang'.

"They said there was these Communists on your waterfront here that was holdin' up the war effort and stopping supplies getting through to our boys. And Russia was the real enemy, and your Government was half-Communist, and we needed to show the people here that the longshoremen was all workin' agin the war effort. So they said I was to flood that hold, and make it look like it was sabotage. The unions would get blamed, and that would show up the Communists for what they was. So I done what they said. I waited till everyone was sent on shore and none below, then in I went. Shoot man, no way was I goin' back to Angola. It's hell there. And then that damn old man stopped me . . . he was tough as an old boot, that feller."

"Old footy player, sport. Waddya reckon?"

"I swam that river, too, an' it was real scary. I could sense them sharks, man, it took forever. I thought I was dead a coupla times. So now I'm deep in the doo-doo. Either way I go down. They might shoot me! Hell, I dunno what to do. Thank god those cullud fellers are watchin' out for me down here. I got a upturned boat to sleep under, and I catch me some catfish – just like home in a way. But they gonna come for me, man. What'll I do?"

"What's your real name?"

"It don't matter none. I ain't been him for a while."

"'You're up shit creek, mate, and gone for all money at this point. I can't see a way clear. You can head down south on the run, there's deserters all over Sydney. Or . . . you can give yourself up.

"Hell no!"

"You're probably right there. Or you can change names again and get on another ship."

"How, man? It ain't like US citizens are just loafin' round lookin' for berths at every port over here."

"No, you'd have to get good papers, and a better story. Which is possible, but I can't do much for ya now. If I sort this business out, I'll send for ya and we'll see what we can do. You're in danger now on a couple of fronts. Lie low, and if I can't get back to ya, a man will come here on the first train from town and sit with his hat upside down on the bench beside him. That'll be the sign. Don't show yourself to anyone else you don't know, and if nobody has come within three days . . . you're on your own."

"It ain't much of a deal."

"It's all there is."

They shook, and Baxter took off down to the end of the platform, then headed off into the scrub that still dripped with dew under the low, muggy sky. Jack sat back down. The train would be a while yet. He rubbed his chin. First they try and sink the cargo, then they hide it, then they sell it, then they want it back bad enough to kill over, but it's all shonky anyway . . .

It didn't add up. He must be missing something, but what was it?

He got out the Doc's pipe.

13

There was no way he was going back to his office; they would still have it staked out. He got off at Vulture Street station and walked up to the phone booth to ring the hotel. Mrs Flowers was there. He didn't muck around.

"You better come and see me. I can't go in there now."

"Why?"

"Look, I found Reg."

"Did you indeed? Where?"

"Not on the phone."

"Very well. I'll come and meet you."

Jack gave her directions, then went back down onto the platform. He stood right up at the end. It was no escape route, it just led to the steep cutting behind Somerville House, and that was no way out. But he couldn't be seen from the street, and that was more important right now. He took another pill, and squatted on his heels to get a mouthful of water from the tap, receiving a disapproving eye from the stationmaster.

He heard footsteps coming down the stairs after half an hour or so, and the sight of her lithe figure tingled his tackle as she stopped at the ticket office and looked around. The hat hung low over her face. He wondered how she was able to manage that movie-star get-up in such short order; most women of his acquaintance took two hours to do the rouge, let alone the whole outfit. She spotted him and walked over.

"Shall we talk here, or go somewhere? I have a car."

"A drive would be nice," he laughed. "It is Sunday."

As they got to street level he saw a Packard sedan pulled up. Jim Simpson was leaning against the mudguard.

Jack stopped. "What's the go here?"

"Get in," said the cop. "And don't worry, you're not gone for a row of shithouses yet."

Jack turned to face her. She looked sheepishly at the ground and fiddled nervously with a hanky.

He couldn't resist it. "Struth, love, you get around."

"Just get in, Jack," Simpson said.

He got into the back seat and they drove silently up Vulture Street towards the cricket ground, then turned up Leopard Street onto River Terrace, and pulled up at the little park at the top of the bluffs.

"Here we are," said Jim, then turned to the couple in the back. "Why don't you two go and have a wee chat?"

They got out and walked to the fence. Other couples were wandering about holding hands; it all looked very domestic.

"What *is* this set-up," he began.

"This is difficult, Jack."

"How so? I did find him, you know."

"Where?"

"In a freezer down the road."

"That's funny, because if you look down there, he's being fished out by the water police as we speak."

He looked over to the other side of the river. There was a boat, and some figures standing around something lying on the mud.

"Well I hope he's thawed out then. Now, you owe me a big

explanation."

"It's over from our point of view."

"Whose point of view? You and me old mate there? Are you an item with him too?"

"Don't be unkind, Jack. I volunteered for this."

"For what?"

She bit her lip, deciding what to say.

He walked back over to the car, exasperated. "Mate, drag ya self outta there and give me the mail on this caper, will ya."

"No, mate," came the reply from inside. "She wants to handle it."

He stormed back over to the fence where the wind was blowing her veil back over her hat.

"Out with it."

"I'm working for Military Intelligence."

"Oh, that's fucken lovely. You're a secret agent."

"I'm a lieutenant, seconded from Signals."

"And your real name?"

"Miriam Connolly."

"So who's the husband? Not bloody Reg, I'll wager!"

"I'm not married."

A tear formed in her eye. It didn't move him.

"Not saving yourself either, eh?"

It was a low blow, but she didn't react.

"There is someone. We couldn't get married, or I would have lost my commission. He was a civilian pilot. He was shot down somewhere over Java just before Singapore fell. I don't know if he's alive or not."

Jack realised what a bastard he sounded like, and pulled his head in. These bloody pills sparked a man up, ya had to watch it.

"Righto, let's go back a tick. Who *is* Reg?"

She relaxed a bit and leant back on the rail.

"A general bad egg from Melbourne, supposedly in the know to quite some extent. Special Branch had him for a load of the stuff in a garage, and it was offered to him as a square-up deal."

"What was offered?"

"To come back up here and find out where the dodgy goods were coming from."

He played dumb. "What dodgy goods?"

"A whole load of second-rate medicines and drugs that's been wreaking havoc in the Fitzroy underworld over the last few weeks."

"How so?"

"Well, there were stabbings by hopheads who'd been stiffed, and various madams carrying on. Two murders we know of. The stuff appeared to have come from here, but any local enquiries were stonewalled by the Yanks. They just didn't want to know. So it was decided that we should do a little bit off our own bat and see what could be turned up. The deal with Reg was, he'd get due consideration in his case if he came up here and jumped up and down till he got some names. He was supposed to report to Jim Simpson, but he vanished after a couple of days. That was when I thought up the idea of pretending to be his wife."

"And Jim sent you my way."

"For security reasons, he was the only local copper who knew what was going on, and he recommended you."

"Gee, I must owe him a favour then . . . Well, where do we go from here?"

He was giving nothing away; the whole thing was riddled with holes. Reg had definitely been closer to this business than they thought, and they'd gone and put the fox back in the hen-house. The less anyone knew about what he knew, the better.

"We'll make a report, and it'll have to go through channels. We've lost our man inside, and that's that."

"Well, no it isn't. What about your dodgy medicine?"

"We've done all we can. It'll have to go HQ and they can sort it out. We've got an informant killed on a highly risky independent investigation, with no result. We'll get our wrists slapped. I'm off the case and going home tonight . . . in disgrace, really."

"Aw, you haven't done too badly."

She looked at him, then turned away to the river.

"That's cruel."

He put his hand out as if to say he was sorry, but drew it back.

"No, I meant the nice hotel, and getting to see the country. But since you mention it . . . What *about* the other night?"

"What about it? You had a good time. You said so."

"Yeah, well. Me manners are a bit rough in the morning. But look . . . I dunno what I'm trying to say."

She gave a short laugh, as you would politely at something that wasn't really funny.

"Well, I probably used you more. It's been rough since Mark disappeared, and I just needed something . . . someone . . ."

"I forgive you."

She smiled, a touch vacantly.

"You want to see me again, is that it?"

"Well, what else?"

"I don't think so, not now. It's too complicated. Until I know what happened to Mark. If he's a prisoner and I betrayed him, I'd never forgive myself . . . Do you understand?"

That explained the no-kissing routine . . . Funny buggers, women.

This was getting messy, and he backed off. "Enough said. I just . . ."

She brightened a bit and stood up straight, although she still looked brittle. "Look me up if you're ever in Melbourne again, or after the war. My parents are in the book: Raven Street, South Yarra."

"You two finished?" said Simpson, as he approached quietly.

"Yep," said Jack. "So I'm off the case?"

"'Fraid so. But tell us what ya know, anyway."

"Someone killed Reg in a freezer full of shonky meat down Stanley Street. And I might have an idea where the medicine came from, but nothin' definite. What more do ya want?"

"That wouldn't be the freezer room where one Arthur Thomas Jones was found with serious head injuries following a robbery, would it? He's not expected to live."

That changed the picture. Simmo knew more than he let on, as usual.

"He must have fallen over as I brushed past him on the way out."

"The Yanks have informed us that you are the individual responsible, but since Jones wasn't exactly a model citizen, I don't really give a rat's arse. If he dies, though, it'll be a different story. I don't know how much I can do for ya then."

"Wait a bloody minute! You put me on the spot in the first place with this charade about the missing husband. What am I supposed to do about that?"

"Nothing. Drop it. You never saw us. Official secrets, defence of the realm, whatever you want to call it."

Jack was fuming. "Mate, half the fucken town knows I've been chasing this Reg clown. Even bloody Darkwell was warning me off, and the Yanks want me run out of town. Thanks for nothin'!"

"We'll pay ya another hundred, then you're on your own. Reg's death means it's a murder investigation now, and it's out of our hands. But he was a no-good, so there won't be too much fuss. It'll settle down. Just keep ya nose clean and lie low."

Jack changed tack. No point getting this lot offside, he had few enough friends as it was.

"You're s'posed to be me mate! I can forgive her, but shit, Jim, you're hanging me out to dry."

It didn't work.

"All's fair in love and war, matey. There's blokes worse off in the jungle."

Fair enough. You tended to forget them sometimes. Jack looked into the distance.

"Anyone else know about this caper?"

"Only some bods up at Vic Barracks. Why?"

"These Yanks aren't pullin' punches. I might need somewhere to run to."

"Forget that. Just keep ya head down and it'll all blow over."

Jack had had enough. He was on his tod, and that was that. Time to get rolling.

"Righto then. Give us a lift down to the Gabba, will ya? I gotta see a mate. It'll keep me out of me usual stamping ground."

"That's the way, sport."

She said nothing.

They got back in the car and drove down to Wellington Road. "This'll do," Jack said.

He jumped out at the corner of Overend Street. As he got out, he shook her hand. "I'll be seeing ya later, I s'pose."

"Perhaps," she replied, as he listened for any hint of emotion. If it was there, it was well hidden.

As they pulled away, Jack felt he was missing her already. That wouldn't do. A beer bottle lay on the footpath. He lined it up and kicked it against a wall, where it smashed, and the sound echoed in the late afternoon silence. It didn't help, and he wished he hadn't done it. Some kid'll step on that. His ribs caught him up and he leant against a lamppost to catch his breath. It had been hard not letting on to her how much pain he was in, but that would have been pissweak. Anyway, he knew where to find sympathy: in the dictionary between shit and syphilis.

14

Some people with small minds thought that any bike made by a legless man couldn't be much chop. Admittedly, you probably wouldn't find Oppy getting around on one, but if you wanted a reliable conveyance that could tangle convincingly with most motor vehicles and come up trumps, then Ridewell was the pushy for you. The small factory was totally run and staffed by limbless vets from the First War, and owned by Jack's old sergeant, Blocker Vinson, who was still a man to be reckoned with, even though the loss of his right leg had ended his footy career. He lived out the back of the works, and since the Broadway on Logan Road would not be open for the arvo session yet, odds on he'd be home. Jack went to the side door and knocked loudly until there was a shouted reply.

"Who's that?"

"Hurry up, brother, the pub's nearly open."

"What's the rush. Wait till I get me leg on."

The door soon opened, and a bear of a man stuck his head out.

"Long time no see."

"Been busy."

They went through the workshop, ducking to avoid the

frames and half-strung wheels dangling from the low ceiling, and into the grimy office at the back. Blocker threw the cat off the pile of *Man* magazines that formed the seat of the chair and sat down.

Jack told enough of the story to get the Blocker's dander up, and then popped the question: "So, can you help us out or what?"

"How?"

"Well I need a tube or two, and some overalls and a bit of wood wool."

"A tube?" replied the big man. "Mate, I have to account for every one of those fucken things, or else the Controller of Tyres can go us for up to a hundred quid."

"Be buggered."

"No, you be buggered. The Japs took Malaya, in case you missed it. The government just brought in tough new rules. The rubber market's tighter than a shark's arse, mate."

"Come on digga. Spare me, will ya."

The big man sat back and swivelled in his chair.

"I s'pose I can swing one."

"Good man, let's get to work then."

They got up and went into the shop, where Blocker handed him a tube and a tin box of used ball bearings.

Jack whipped out his blade, trimmed the tube to about a yard, then tied a knot in one end. He filled the tube carefully with the greasy little steel balls, squeezing them down like he was packing a sausage, until there was a decent fifteen inches neatly loaded in, slightly stretching the rubber without making it too rigid. He then tied another knot, looped about another nine inches over, then tied that off, making a handle that would grip on itself with pressure.

He held up the persuader and admired it. It was so much

more effective than a steel bar: easier to hide, wouldn't break any bones (just inflict gruesome internal bruising), nasty to be on the receiving end of, and very handy in an uneven match-up.

"Oo-er," said Blocker, "I'm glad you won't be swingin' that *my* way."

"Too right, me old brown son. But some bastard's coppin' it before the night's out, be sure of that."

Blocker threw him a pair of overalls; the dirty khaki would pass for a uniform from a distance. They went out to the dispatch area, where there were a few crates full of timber shavings, tied off the arms and legs with string, and began to fill them with the packing material.

"Just like a sniper decoy, old sport," laughed the Blocker, "Tally ho!"

The truck was old but the livery was in good order and it still looked pretty swish; Jack admired it as he turned the crank. No one would look twice at it in an industrial area. The engine finally fired up and the lamps flickered into life.

They trundled off into the evening gloom. As they went down Stanley Street towards the bridge over the creek, Jack climbed into the back and grabbed the dummy, ready to jump out the side door.

They turned into Cavendish Road, then round the corner again, and along past the warehouse. Jack could see a staff car parked inside the fence. Blocker kept going to the end of the road, turned around and came back to pull up opposite. Jack crept out of the truck and into the gap between two warehouses, then quickly pulled the dummy in behind the bush that grew from the corner. Keeping out of the cone of light thrown by the streetlight, he whistled lightly. Blocker couldn't hear him over the rumble of the idling motor, so Jack had to throw a rock against the running board to signal him to go. As the truck pulled away, Jack peered out from the darkness: no one could be seen. He'd been perfectly planted. Now to lie doggo and see who turned up.

He pulled out his old railway watch. An hour had passed with no sign of life from inside the building, but he didn't want to go in and be caught on the hop. Enough of that; it was his turn to have the jump.

He heard the jeep shortly before its headlights swung into the street, so he waited until it stopped to allow one of them to open the gate, then get back in and go up the driveway. He swiftly dragged the straw man out to the bottom of the light pole and propped it up so it looked as if someone was sitting there, half in shadow. He put his hat on its head and then pressed himself back against the edge of the building, out of the light on the footpath that was dappled by the leaves of the frangipani tree.

As soon as the jeep motor was turned off, Jack rolled an empty beer bottle out onto the road and yelled, "Assholes!"

It worked. Without going inside, both MPs turned and started walking back down the drive and across the road towards the decoy. They realised something was wrong from about ten feet away, but still went right over to it.

"What's this goddamn nonsense?" he heard as he waited for his moment.

It came quickly. One of them bent over to take the hat off as the other looked up and down the street. He had him lined up like a penalty kick in a grand final. Two steps around and he planted his boot right under Chuck's chin, sending him over like a sack of spuds, as he swung the persuader in a arc from the left that caught the other one right across the side of the bonce.

Frank staggered, and Jack followed with another blow across the back of his head as he stumbled into the grass verge, out on his feet. He went back to Chuck and dragged him by the armpits over to the lamppost. He used their own handcuffs to lock them together with their arms around the pole. It had all taken a minute at most.

Jack rubbed his ribs then picked up a rock and flung it upwards, knocking out the light. This was work best done in the dark; he couldn't have their mates cottoning on yet. He waited until they both started to come around, then stuffed their ties in their mouths before they made too much noise.

"Well now, fellers, gotchers a beauty with that one, eh? Ya know, I was gunna ask yez a few questions, but I can't be fucked. It just looks like a case of six of the best to me."

He began to swing the rubber tube in wide arcs into the shackled men: across the shoulders and into the kidneys, but avoiding their heads. One good turn deserved another. He kept flailing away, blow after blow, like a woodchopper at the Ekka, until his ribs couldn't take any more. He wiped away the sweat running down his face. These blokes would remember this for a while, and maybe think twice next time they decided to dish it out on some other poor bastard. They weren't out for the count, but they were not too chipper. As he dusted off his hat and put it on, he leant over.

"Mind how ya go, fellers. Next time I'll get nasty."

Tucking their pistols into his belt, he strolled through the open gate to the jeep, where he pulled the magazine out of the Thompson and threw it into the dark. Then he slowly opened the warehouse door. The man tied to the post inside was looking down at the space behind the door as best he could without appearing to. Jack took the hint. He slammed the door all the way open, and whoever was behind copped it. Then he slammed it again and again until the body fell out. It was his old mate Tremayne, the glamour boy. This was as good as Christmas.

He took the man's belt and tied his hands behind him with it.

"They gonna torch this place, man," said Sergeant King as Jack cut him loose, "and me with it. These Klan muthafuckas don't change wherever they is."

He was right. There was a strong smell of petrol, and several wires led to various bits of ordinance.

"Better call your superiors, mate," he offered.

"They ain't gonna listen to me, man, I'm gone. You handle it. They might listen to you." He stopped and turned, "Thanks, I owe ya." Then he bolted into the night.

Jack rubbed his chin. He'd best be making himself scarce too, but not before satisfying his curiosity. He ripped back the tarpaper on one of the pallets and opened the first bandage pack he saw. It was just cotton trash and rags: no use to anybody. He tried a field dressing: same thing. The whole bloody joint was full of this, and it was all shit. He looked closely at a tin of foot powder. *Manufactured by Tremanco Med. Larkville, Tenn.*

The penny dropped with a mighty clang.

He slapped Tremayne around the face and lifted him to his feet.

"We're goin' for a walk, sport, and you'll tell me the whole story."

He came to as Jack lifted him up and started struggling. A quick swipe with the persuader stopped that, but he started laughing.

"You don't know what's going on here, buddy. You best save your ass now and let me go."

"Fuck that! You're gunna talk."

"Like hell!"

"You don't know what the fucken word means. I've been there, and fairies like you didn't last, lemme tell ya. Now walk or be fucken dragged."

Grabbing some of the rope hanging from the chair, he pushed Tremayne out the door and into the jeep, shoving his arms over the back of the seat so that the lashing held him tight, and in pain.

"That hurts, asshole!"

"Good. That's the idea."

He drove out and around the station, then into Gladstone Street and down onto Main Avenue, then pulled up under the bridge.

"What's this, pal?"

Jack dragged him out of the jeep.

"You'll see."

He punched Tremayne hard in the guts, doubling him up so he could re-tie his arms in front of him, then grabbed the rest of the rope and dragged the gasping officer up the embankment to where it met the bridge. He threw the rope over the rail and down into the gap between the sleepers, then pulled it back through so that he could drag Tremayne over the rail to whatever point he deemed fit.

Jack pulled out one of the .45s and pointed it at Tremayne's head.

"Right, start ya story."

"I ain't talkin'. You won't shoot me."

"Don't bet on it," Jack hissed. Then he paused for a minute, as if puzzled by this seemingly obvious fact. "But you might be right, it wouldn't look good. However, you getting both your arms chopped off by the train which is picking up passengers about a mile down the track as we speak . . . Well now, that could be mere carelessness if you looked at it the right way."

The Yank twisted his head to the right and looked down the track. Sure enough, at the point where the shiny rails met in the moonlit distance there was a train, and it started moving towards them.

"You wouldn't dare."

"You don't think so, eh? Let's see then."

He pulled down hard on the rope and stretched Tremayne over the rail until his feet were nearly off the ground and his head and shoulders were right on the metal. Then he braced himself against the stanchion.

The train got closer.

"You're kidding, right?" Tremayne grunted helplessly as he kicked and scuffled his feet to try and get some traction.

"No I'm not, young feller me lad. More than one Jerry died for not talkin' quick enough when I took a fancy to it, so don't fool yaself."

The train got to the bridge, and the thrumming and rattling built to a crescendo as the engine closed in. It was barely a carriage length from them when Jack let go of the rope. Tremayne pulled his arms out and fell back, tumbling halfway down the slope as the thundering carriages shook the bridge overhead. Jack slid down after him and grabbed the rope.

"That was just a taste. Back up we go."

"Hold it, hold it. Okay, man, I'll tell ya."

"That's better. Now you tell me everything, there's a good chap!"

The whole cargo was fake. The contractors in the States knew that overproduction was the name of the game, and there were warehouses full of all sorts of materiel as backup that would probably never be used. So all the company had to do was turn out fake product and bung it in storage, banking on the fact that it would never actually be needed. The leftover raw materials were then shipped on to other wholesalers, or used in other lines. Huge profits resulted.

A great scheme, until some clerk copied down a number wrong and a fleet of trucks arrived to cart off a whole shipment of the wrong boxes. Then it was panic time. The cargo was followed across America, and all sorts of ruses were tried, but it had become a part of the system and had its own momentum. By the time it got to Long Beach to be loaded, it was too late. Desperate measures were considered, but there was no way to stop the boat at this point. Security was too tight to try anything there. But their tentacles spread wide: they heard that a sailor from the ship in question had been picked up with a possible false identity. Palms were greased, and the idea of flooding the hold in Brisbane – to write off the goods and throw everybody off the scent – was dreamed up.

"Who came up with that idea?" Jack asked.

"My pop."

"Him being the boss of this here Tremanco, the defence manufacturer."

"That's right."

"So your only justification for wearing that uniform is as a jumped up sales rep for daddy's firm."

"Hey, I'm an important go-between for the industry."

"Fuck me roan, what a war! Righto then, I've figured out how you got the stuff to the warehouse over the road there . . . then what?"

"We were gonna just leave it there nice and quiet, with a few nigra boys to watch over it, till we could figure somethin' out, do one of them jewboy stocktakes maybe."

"Which was all set up just now, and the sarge was going up with it as well."

"Well hey, a nice quiet bit of goldbrickin' ain't good enough for them lazy assholes. Oh no, they gotta start sellin' the stuff on the black market. 'Cause of course *they* don't know the stuff's no good, the greedy dumb fucks. Next thing we got all sorts of shit comin' from all over, and we're payin' this guy and that guy . . . goddammit, everybody's got his hand out in this jerk-water town, it's worse than Chicago!"

"So you find out who's selling the stuff, and just shoot them out of hand like animals."

"They *are* fucken animals, man! You don't know."

"So the rape story was all bullshit."

"Just some hooker we paid to kick up a fuss."

"So they never raped anybody."

"Who cares? They would if they could. Ya need that kinda shit as a warning, buddy. We got to keep our foot on their necks real hard or else they gonna jump up and bite us, y'hear."

"What about Reg? He was a white man."

"Hey now, don't blame us for that! We told that fat bozo to rough 'im up and see who knew what, but the boys swear he was still alive when they left that meat-hall, and that's the truth."

"You'd kill Baxter if ya got hold of him."

"No need. He'll go back on the chain gang when we find him. No-one'll believe a story like that from a white-trash geek like him. Anyway, he suckered up all that shit we fed him like a total fool. What a patsy! Although them Com'nists really *are* all over the place here. You better watch y'selves."

Tremayne was now regaining his sass, and Jack looked at him quizzically.

"You will, ah, repeat all this to the proper authorities when I take ya into central, won't you."

"Who are you kiddin', man? I got connections. This won't raise an eyebrow anywhere. We got pals all the way to the top."

"You murdered two of your own men."

"Wise up, fool! We shoot niggers for all sorts of reasons . . .

Ain't nobody gonna give a shit, believe me. Are we finished? Can I go now?"

A train whistle hooted, and Jack grabbed the rope. He dragged Tremayne back up the embankment kicking and protesting.

"Whatcha doin'? Hey, back off!"

"Nah, not tonight."

The train got closer, and Jack socked him on the thigh with the persuader, dropping him with the pain, cut the rope holding his hands together, then twisted his arm behind him, and forced his head onto the rail. It was vibrating louder and louder and Tremayne began screaming.

"Shit, man, what are ya doing!"

"Seeing if ya can die like a man."

The more he struggled, the harder Jack twisted his arm. The train was right on top of them in a cloud of steam, and Jack pulled back just enough for the first wheel to grind past Tremayne's head, then pushed him forward again until his nose was being brushed by the steel and starting to bleed.

The roar of the clashing steel was louder than a foundry, but he could still hear Tremayne wailing like a lost soul among the swirling cinders, screaming his heart out in utter terror.

The guard's van was well past before he became aware of an acrid smell halfway between spew and off meat. He'd smelt it before, on the killing floors and in the trenches. It was the smell of shit from deep within, when a man or beast loses his arse in fear or death, and every last drop pours out of him. Once smelt, forever known and not forgotten. Tremayne had filled his daks like a one-year-old, and lay sobbing at his feet.

Jack kicked him.

"What are ya, mate? You're a fucken disgrace to your uniform."

He kicked Tremayne again as he rolled down the slope to the

slimy pool at the bottom. Jack stood over him in contempt. He hated spivs and bludgers. Milking things for their own advantage when good men were dying to keep the bastards safe at home.

He pulled out the Colt and cocked it, then pointed it at the prone figure.

"Say your fucken prayers, sport."

A flashlight beam caught him in the eye.

"Hold ya horses."

He knew the voice; it was Simpson.

"Mate, don't do it. You'll hang for it, and this germ isn't worth swinging for."

Jack hesitated long enough to be dramatic, then threw the gun to the ground.

"He's right, unfortunately, you turd. You're not worth it. Fuck ya. Get outta me sight."

He walked over to Simpson and gave him the other .45 as headlights from arriving vehicles lit up the scene.

"Where'd you spring from?"

"Mate, I might *look* silly."

Several figures in various uniforms were approaching the scene by now. The game was obviously up all round.

"How'd you find us?"

"Flanagan here's not as thick as he looks, either. When a report came in from a nightwatchman down the road about some joker whacking the shit out of some Yank MPs, he called me, figuring it might be related to your visit to the knocking shop."

"Who told ya 'bout that?"

"We miss nothin'. Anyway, then he remembered your interest in those spooks getting shot down here, plus a report from some local mum about her boys seeing some bloke getting beat up by MPs in the same spot. We called the cavalry and got down here chop chop . . . and a good thing too, by the look of it. You're a very bad man when ya get worked up."

"Who, me? Nah, the bastard'll talk now anyway."

"No I won't." With a hysterical laugh, Tremayne leapt up from the mud, the discarded Colt in his hand.

"Put that down, sir!" came an American voice from the side. Jack could see MPs with their guns out.

"Sir, put down the weapon."

An officer stepped into the headlights.

"We know it all, Tremayne. The game's up. Let's go, feller."

"You know nothing!" he shouted. The gun, trembling in his hands, threw shadows on the grey timber of the bridge pylons.

The officer tried again. "We've found all the stuff. Give yourself up."

"Hell no! Get over here, you."

He gestured at Jack, who stood his ground.

"Piss off, mate. Ya stink."

"I'll kill you, goddamn it."

"Fair enough, have a go."

"Sir, for the last time, put the weapon down!"

Tremayne brought the gun up at Jack and pulled the trigger, just as a burst of automatic fire from above threw him over one of the crossbeams. He hung there for a second like a rag doll, then slid down the post, his blood mixing with the dark collar of creosote at his feet.

As more Americans arrived and clustered around the body, Jack and Simpson leaned back on the bonnet of his car.

"Smoke?' said Simpson.

"Nah, I just wanna go home. I've been doing your dirty work for too long this weekend. I need a lie down."

"That was pretty cool-headed stuff back there with that maniac. Ya coulda got shot."

"If it was loaded, I mighta."

Simpson cackled as he leaned inside the car and pulled out a flask.

"You're a fucken character."

"I'll drink to that."

An American officer walked over to them.

"Okay, guys, we'll take this from here. You've had your fun."

Simpson laughed and pointed his flask at Jack.

"He's had all the fun. All I did was make phone calls."

"Well let's just say that in the interests of Allied co-operation the whole matter will be thoroughly investigated, and we thank you for it."

Simpson looked quizzically at the American.

"Brothers in arms, eh?"

The officer smirked as he tipped his hat, then walked back to his car and barked, "Back to the warehouse."

"Yass Sir!" snapped the driver. The Buick threw up a spray of gravel as it turned right in front of them.

Simpson screwed the top back on the flask.

"Well, we've done our bit. We better go into town and make a statement to keep the record straight from our end. Although this'll all be hushed up like that big barney in town last year, no doubt."

"What about the two blackfellers they done in down here?"

"What about 'em, sport? There's people dying every day and everywhere. Forget it."

"Easy to say."

"And easier to do, mate. There's a war on, things happen. Ya did what ya could. Ya can't save the world."

"Yeah, that's the Yanks' job, it appears."

'Well, let 'em do it. Anyway, paperwork calls. Got all night, have ya?"

"Looks that way."

A dull roar could be heard in the distance as a heavy shower pounded the roofs of Coorparoo. It was heading their way.

They got in the car.

15

MONDAY

It had been a long night, and Jack was still sparking from the bloody pills, but he knew he was going to go down like tall timber before very long. There was one thing to tidy up, though. He got off the tram in West End and walked into a little shop with a dusty window. A sad-looking lady passed him in the doorway stuffing some notes into her purse. An old man walked back out to the counter.

"Sol, I need a guitar."

"You becoming a singer now, mister Jack?"

"Yeah sure. Ya got one?"

The old man pulled something out from the shelves that stretched away into the back of the shop.

"This is very nice piece for you, mister Jack, from Spain."

He looked at it. The varnish was worn, and the paper decal inside the body was flaking.

"Bit long in the tooth, isn't it?"

"But a good one, I assure you."

"Righto, how much?"

"For you," he paused and sucked his remaining front tooth. "Sixty pounds."

"What! It'd have to boil water as well for that kinda money."

"No, mister Jack, this is a fine instrument. Try it."

He strummed the open strings: it did have a warm tone, but really, what did he know?

"Look, Sol, I just haven't got that kind of dough."

"Alright, for you . . . fifty, but that's my final price! I'm tellink you: this is no rubbish I sell you."

"Fifty, eh? Well how 'bout we set a price on the next time your no-good son-in-law comes round and starts breaking things and puttin' the acid on ya to cover his turf losses, and you need me to have a quiet word to 'im out back?"

"Of course. Forgive me, mister Jack. I'm always thinking business first. You are my friend. Here, you take this . . . it is yours."

"Hang on, I'm no fucken standover man. Just give us a fair price."

"Very well," he sighed. "You decide what is fair."

Jack threw twenty-five quid on the table while Sol unrolled a length of shiny brown paper from under the guillotine.

When the string was tied and cut, he picked it up and smiled at the old man.

"That's more mately, isn't it? You send for me if that prick comes round again."

As he put on his hat in the doorway, he turned. "Ya know, ya shoulda told me that daughter of yours was gunna marry outside the faith. I mighta threw me hat in the ring."

"A man like you for a son would make me glad, but looking back is easy, mister Jack – you see where the trouble was hiding. But to look forward and see it. God doesn't seem to want this."

"Yours maybe. I haven't asked my bloke. See ya, Sol."

He stepped out into the sunlight and walked over to the tram stop.

The cicadas were louder than a sawmill as Jack walked up the stairs of the house of ill-repute.

The girls were doing their washing in the copper downstairs; some of it was already propped up on the line out the back.

"You're early, big fella," said one.

"Not today, sweetheart. I've been in the wars."

"Who hasn't? We can fix that."

"Boss lady in?" he asked as he got to the top of the stairs.

"Whattya want?" came her reply from the doorway. "We're shut, and you've caused enough trouble."

"Is that young Leroy fella still about?"

"He's not here now, so hop it."

"Look, just see that he gets this and you'll never see me again."

A huge form filled the space behind her. The sergeant.

'Watchew want with him?"

The look they gave each other stopped any discussion of the night before.

"Well, I sorta liked that blues stuff he was doin', and I figured this . . . well, you know."

The big man took it and put it behind the door.

"He'll get it."

"If he ever does any recordings when he gets home, you tell him to send me one, alright? Here's my address."

"Okay, mister."

He winced as they shook hands, and the sergeant said quietly, "You done enough, friend. Go easy on yourself."

Jack grunted as the shock of his foot hitting the first stair back down went through him.

"Yeah, I'm about done in. See ya later."

It was time to go home. He stopped at the bottom and looked back up.

"Shit, one last detail. What are we going to do about Baxter?"

"He's gone, man."

"Where? Did they pick him up?"

"Hell, I dunno. One of the boys went down there, but there was no sign of him, and them local fellers didn't know anything or wouldn't say. I hope he's away clean, but it's up to him now, whatever happens."

"Well I didn't tell 'em where he was, so if they got him, someone else squawked. But like you say, he might have gone south. Not much I can do about it either way. I'm pulling up stumps on this caper. You take care now."

He stopped for a second. Bloody hell, he was starting to talk like these bastards. Best steer clear of 'em in future.

16

MONDAY NIGHT

The best thing about the old chip heater was that once you got it going, you could have a virtually endless hot shower. The benzedrine had worn off, and Jack lay back on his bed, fully prepared to go nowhere for a week. Vida came in and gasped when she saw the bruises. She knelt on the floor beside the bed.

"You look like ya need a bit of private nursing there."

"Aw, I'm a bit stiff right now."

"Promises, promises." She patted his knee and stood up.

"Another call came from Melbourne while you were in that shower for so long, but I wouldn't take it."

"Did they say who it was?"

"No."

"Fuck 'em then. Had enough trouble from down that way for the moment."

"Want anything?"

"Yeah, can you crank up the gramophone for us?"

"Sure, love. And I'll bring in some soup later."

"Christ, don't remind me."

"What?"

"Oh, nothin'. This'll do for now," he said, taking another

113

mouthful from the ice-cold largie on the bedside table and re-placing the match on the neck.

The perfect strains of Joe Loss's "Begin the Beguine" filled the room as he scraped a bit more of the dark tar from the little bottle and smeared it into the pipe.

He'd have to chase down some of that blues stuff, too. He couldn't see Paling's carrying any, but ya never know.

Chick Henderson's voice soared to that classic high note at the end as Jack lay back smiling. Fruit bats squabbled in the tree outside the window as a light rain tickled the tin roof.

A man could get used to this stuff.

THE IRISH FANDANGO

1

A dust devil whirled in the chill of the westerly gust as he walked, hunched over, down Stanley Street. It wasn't what you'd call winter in other parts of the world, but it was chilly enough. A man oughta get a bloody heater for the office, he thought, as a newspaper wrapped itself around his leg, and he shook it off before climbing the steps. Could be worse, though . . . A man could be stuck in Stalingrad eating horsemeat – or your mates, come to that.

The gilt-lettered JM INVESTIGATIONS on the glass door was peeling, and the office was sparsely furnished, but it was still a damn sight better than wandering around outside.

Things were slow: a couple of domestic hanky-pankies had kept the rent paid, but the last one had been a fizzer. The bastards had made up, and having joined forces again, wouldn't pay. He monstered 'em a bit, but behind the flash front they put up they were just battlers, and it wasn't worth the effort.

The phone rang. He spun his legs off the desk and leaned forward to take the call. It was his wharfie mate Len, asking him to come down to the Valley for a beer. They went way back and were good mates, but Len was a right commo when it came down to it, and that was one thing Jack wasn't. So they rarely discussed politics at drinking time, which was usually later than this.

Jack wasn't really in the mood.

"Mate, booze for breakfast is the sure sign of a dipso. Besides, I haven't got two bob to scratch me arse with."

"You insult me, cobber. When did you ever go short of the necessities if I was around? And this is about work, anyway, ya miserable coot."

"Sorry, digga. It's this cold weather, puts the spite in a man's bones."

"Yeah well, shove ya bad manners back in the bottom drawer and drag ya carcass down to the Imperial. It'll be open by the time ya show."

The office workers had all bundied on by now, so Jack had no trouble getting a seat, and he pulled his coat tightly around him to keep out the draughts that came through the centre section as the tram trundled across the Vic Bridge, past two lonesome-looking Navy men staring at the water through the iron trellis. They had that last-day-on-leave look; one threw his cigarette into the water far below as he turned and looked blankly at the passing traffic.

The desperates were already nursing glasses in their own little columns of smoke as Jack undid his coat and sat down at the table in the corner, where Len sat beside another man in an overcoat. Three glasses on the table meant the ordering was already done, so he sat straight down.

"Righto, so what's worth draggin' a man from his considered repose this brisk mornin'?"

"Meet Clancy O'Dea," Len said.

O'Dea was a sour-looking bastard with round glasses perched on the end of his thin nose – like a teacher, or something else bookish. Jack didn't take to him from the off, but he kept it polite, grunting "Ow ya goin'."

"Well, comrade, and you?"

Right, he thought, another bloody Red. Oh well, takes all kinds.

Len broke the awkward pause. "Clancy here is lookin' for a discreet sort of bloke to make a few enquiries for 'im."

Jack smirked slightly. "Is that right? The wife misbehavin' on ya, champ?"

"I'm married to the cause, comrade."

Jack looked quizzically at Len, whose brow was similarly dark.

"Can we speak freely here?" Clancy whispered.

Len guffawed. "No fizgigs in here, me old brown son!"

"You sure of that? 'Cause I'm not!" Jack offered. "Half these urgers in 'ere'd shoot their mother for sixpence. I'm off, this smells."

Len was right on it; he could read the wind. "Hold ya horses. Let's knock these back and go for a walk. The park'll look nice this early."

The details flowed a bit more freely out in the open air as they strolled down Brunswick Street, and by the time they got to New Farm Park Jack had the mail. Len's new mate was a Communist official – no organisation was actually named, but that's what Jack assumed. One of their members had hung himself the week before, or so the police claimed, and Clancy and his pals were in need of a bit more convincing about that, given their past relationships with the organs of the law. Jack wondered if they knew he'd been a copper, and decided it didn't matter if they did. It was the job that concerned them now, and as he always stated, a professional is someone who can do something he hates, for those he despises, really well, if the money's good.

That was all there was to it.

"So what do you want me to do?" he asked, without committing himself.

"Just check it out. We wanna know why a bloke just up and tops himself without leaving at least a note. It doesn't sit right. Bill was doin' alright, as far as we knew. Had just paid his dues. Somethin's fishy."

Jack rubbed his chin. "Len, over here."

They walked away from the serious one.

"What's this fucken caper, mate?" You better not be settin' me up with some sort of commo conspiracy here. I don't need fucken bombthrowers in me life."

"Mate, it's a breeze, you'll piss it in. Anyway, what are ya worried about? The ban's been lifted; they're legit."

"Yeah, that's this week. I don't need to get mixed up in political squabbles."

"No one's askin' for any favours here, sport. The brothers pay well, and whattya you care? We're all on the same side in this show, aren't we?"

Apparently so, given the titanic struggle the Red Army was putting up against the Teutonic hordes, even though they'd been best mates not that long ago. As far as Jack could see, nothing was a given with political types.

"Alright then, but this better not jump up and bite me on the arse. I've got a reputation, ya know."

Len shook his head. "Struth, I've heard it all now . . . Your name's mud, ya fucken drongo! Ya oughta thank a man for sendin' ya cushy numbers like this one. Here's the address, and fifty smackers for two days diggin' . . . and there's more in the tit. Moscow gold, matey, all ya can handle. Make the most of it!"

Len was right. Jack was a shit-stirrer from way back, even if he wasn't particularly Socialist or Trotskyite or whatever the fuck they called themselves. He looked at the serious figure standing off to the side, and mulled it over . . . Bugger the powers that be: money's money. But that clown will be the first one to cop a flogging if this all goes west.

Jack put his hand out: he liked to do things against his better judgment sometimes, just for fun.

2

It wasn't a steep pull up the hill from the wharves, but it was long enough, and by the time Jack reached the top of Vulture Street he was a touch puffed, if glad of the warmth from the exercise. The morning was bright and intense, and the angle of the winter sun sharply delineated the hills in the distance. He couldn't see forever, but far enough to make him stop and take it all in for a second before his mind refocused on matters at hand.

The flat was upstairs in an old mansion divided into four, and the grounds were more than reasonably tidy. This Bill character wasn't doing too much struggling on behalf of the masses, by the look of it. The key was under the mat and he was letting himself in when the proverbial old dear next door stuck her head out.

"Can I help you?"

"Yeah. I'm a distant cousin of Bill's, and the family sent me round to get a few things."

"Wouldn't his wife do that?"

His ears pricked up; no one had said anything about a Mrs Callaghan. He tap-danced.

"Um, she's at her mum's place."

"Back in Spain? How did she do that? Wouldn't it be a bit

dangerous?"

This was getting tricky. The old bat knew far more than he did.

"Um, I'm not sure. I thought they'd moved here. As I said, I'm from a distant branch of the family; I haven't seen Bill since we were kids. I was just asked to do what I can while I'm in town . . . the war, you know."

That worked; she softened. "Isn't it terrible? You know, I didn't think her leaving would affect him so."

This might be the easiest fifty Jack would ever earn.

"She left, did she?"

"Oh yes, some months back. I think there might have been some other chap, but one didn't like to ask too much."

I bet, he thought. This one missed very little, by the sound of it. Best butter her up.

"Look, I won't be long. It's a bit of a grim duty, if you know what I mean. You wouldn't have a cup of tea for a returned man after I've finished would you?"

"Why of course," she smiled. "We'll take it here on the veran-dah like I did with William from time to time." She shook her head. "Nice chap, you know, dreadful waste."

There wasn't much to show for a death scene. The rooms were full of books on shelves made of butter boxes. The stuff you'd expect: Marx, Lenin, Stalin . . . and a whole bunch of blokes he'd never heard of: Nietzsche, Feuerbach, Kierkegaard, god knows who else. This bloke must have liked a serious read, so he can't have been a nong. There were rope marks on the archway in the hall, although he couldn't help thinking that even allowing for the eleven-foot ceiling, the bugger can't have been too far off the ground. Still, as long as the toes aren't touching . . . out ya go.

He went into the bedroom. Nothing out of the ordinary there, except for a couple of battered photo-frames lying face down. He picked one of them up; it showed a man in a leather coat, unshaven, wearing a forage cap and bandolier. It didn't require the *Cantina* sign over the shoulder of the raven-haired beauty on his arm to work out the time and place. The Spanish Civil War had been over for nearly four years, but the images weren't easily forgotten. Bill Callaghan must have been in the International Brigades, and it was odds on the girl was the missus.

There was more to this than met the eye, as usual, and he chuckled, couldn't help himself. He knew one thing: politics was always a messy business, where nothing was what it seemed. He went back to the main room and rummaged about on the desk, then went straight to the bottom drawer and opened it. It was a jumble of papers and odd bits of shit like old pen nibs and baccy tins full of gramophone needles, but right at the back was the torn half of a photograph. He pulled it out of the mess and held it up to the light peeping through the blinds.

It was an old school photo, depicting a few boys and what was presumably their teacher, though only a black-clad arm laid across the shoulders of one lad could be seen on this side of the tear. In the background was a palm tree in front of an old lace-ironwork balcony, and a gatepost bearing the name of the school. Jack had never heard of St Aloysius, but that meant little: he'd suffered a variety of tortures at the hand of some nuns for one term in Grade 3, and had made a point of keeping a long way from anything to do with the Catholic Church and its minions ever since. He put the torn photo in the pocket of his jacket, then went back into the bedroom and pulled back the cover of the bed. No snail trails, so the old dear was apparently right: there'd only been one bod on that mattress recently. He picked up the other photo from the bedside table; it was a colour portrait of the wife, and her ruby lips and green eyes made him think about life and death for a minute. There was no way any sensible bloke would top himself over this piece, gorgeous as she was – indeed, just the fact that he'd been her man at *any* time would be reason enough to keep going, Jack would have thought. An educated feller might think on a loftier plane than an old pants man, however. Time would tell.

The winter sun through the bougainvillea dappled the boards on the verandah as he took his tea, and Myrtle kept up the chatter as he sipped. She was a cluey old bird and sent one over as soon as the pleasantries had been exhausted.

"You're not a relative at all, are you?"

He decided to play a straight bat.

"No, not really. But I am acting on behalf of people who cared about him."

"I knew it! And you're not the police."

"How do you know?"

"You must forgive an old fusspot, Mr . . . ?"

"Munro, Jack Munro."

"Well, they've already been. And forgive me, Jack, if I may call you that, but you're a bit too debonair to be a policeman."

That was a funny way to look at things. "I used to be," Jack replied.

"That may be so. If it is, then the change is definitely for the better."

Bloody hell, the old bugger was flirting with him. Better oil it up a bit.

"You must have been quite a belle in your day as well."

She flushed and wiggled in her cane chair, then composed herself. "Enough of the flattery, young man. Did you find what you came for?"

"I dunno. Perhaps."

"That's rather vague, what do these friends of Bill's want you to do."

This was getting too direct: she had him on the spot now. He started back-pedalling.

"Just check on the arrangements, you know."

"But the Church are handling all that."

He made sure not to react. "That's good of them . . . how did they get involved?"

"It was a priest who found him. He called the police."

"Is that right?"

"Yes indeed. Mind you, he was in there for quite a while before he went and called them from the box on the corner. He must have been praying for him or something, whatever they do. I'm a Lutheran myself, you know."

This was a bit too neat. Jack's nose started twitching, but he kept his composure.

"So the priest was here before the police, not the other way round?"

"That's right."

"Well how did he get in?"

"I'm sure I don't know. I didn't really give it much thought. Maybe he had a key, like you."

She was sharp as a tack.

"So he'd been here before?"

"He may have been. I'm sure I couldn't say."

She'd gone a bit cagey, but he kept at it anyway.

"And the police didn't seem too concerned about it?"

"Not that I noticed."

"Did they ask you about it?"

"Not as such, no."

"Did they ask you anything?"

"Not really, just the usual."

"What's the usual, may I ask? Are you often questioned by

the police?"

She bridled at that. "I've been to the pictures, you know. I know how they do it. He just asked where the wife was, when did I see him last, and that's about it . . . *As it is for you*, young man! I don't like your manner any more."

He'd played the hand too hard. Time to go.

"One last question," he said as he put on his hat, thinking of the old-boy angle.

"Did the policeman mention his name?"

"Which one?"

"The constable taking your statement."

"It was an inspector, I'll have you know," she sniffed. "O'Reilly, I believe. Good *day*!"

O'Reilly – that bastard! They'd crossed paths before, and Jack screwed up his face at the memory of it.

As he went down the stairs, his mind was racing. This bloke was a Red so what was a bloody priest doin' there? As far as he knew the commos went round dynamiting churches whenever possible . . . And why the hell would O'Reilly turn up at a simple suburban suicide.

Blind Freddy could see the answer to that. Because it wasn't.

3

By the time Jack had got down to the stop on Stanley Street, waited for a tram and then ridden it back to South Brissie station, he'd got the workings of a plan. He jumped on a West End tram as it slowed through the intersection, and got off a few stops later outside Sol's hock shop.

"How's it goin', me old mate?" he greeted the old man as he came out at the ringing of the tarnished bell over the door.

"I'm alive. What can I help you with, my friend?"

"Mate, I need a lens for me camera, one that does real close up stuff – a magnifier or something."

"You becomink a spy perhaps, mister Jack?"

"Nah, fuck that malarky. I just need a real close shot on a photo, so I can get some detail."

"Yours is a Zeiss, I'm recalling?"

"That's what ya sold me."

"They make such beautiful things, the Germans, yet they have wolves in their souls. Such a pity."

"It's more than a fucken pity, sport, they're a pack o' bastards. I know, I've killed a few."

He rarely said anything like that, and he pulled himself up; they both fell silent as the old man handed him the lens.

"This will do the job. Forty pounds."

"You'll break me, y'old bastard. Look, how about I borrow it for a week? Here's a fiver."

The old man's face scrunched up as he did his sums.

"But Jack, what if some fellow comes in and wants to buy this thing? I lose thirty-five!"

"Get off the grass, you old dingo. The bloody thing's got more dust on it than the Birdsville track! It'll still be here when we're both dead."

"Such a bargainer . . . Ay, if I had a son like you."

"Speaking of the family, how's the daughter these days?"

"I could tear my beard out the way that pig treats my daughter. He was sent to punish me, this one. He hits her now, I'm sure. She won't say, but a father knows these things."

Jack arced up.

"Any man who hits a woman isn't one, for my money. You give me the address, I'll go round and belt that prick so hard he'll be shitting teeth til doomsday. Just say the word."

"Please, my friend. I have enough trouble already. I know you mean well."

"I'm fair dinkum. I'll bash the cunt."

"That's my worry, my friend."

Jack realised he'd scared Sol and backed off. The old bloke probably had enough grief without him storming into it. A quiet word was one thing, a good flogging something else again.

He handed over a blue one and pocketed the lens.

"See ya in a week. mate."

As he got to the door he turned and asked, on a whim. "Mate, do you recall that guitar ya sold us a few months back?"

"Of course."

"Where'd it come from?"

"Spain."

"Yeah, I meant how did you get it?"

"From a Spaniard, of course."

He went back to the counter.

"A few of them about, is there?"

"Not so many around here, just a few refugees from the war, but many more working up in the canefields, I believe."

"Do they hang about anywhere in particular?"

"There is a small hall down near the river where they sometimes have dances and cook their food. Too much pork on the menu for my liking, I'm told, but some very fine fellows. Why do you ask?"

Jack fished out the picture of Mrs Callaghan.

A smile lit up the shopkeeper's face. "I should have guessed."

"Seen this one about by any chance?"

"Maybe. I don't look too hard these days."

"Don't give me that shit, you old perv. Let me know if you do."

"My eye is like an eagle for you, mister Jack."

"Good man."

He stepped out into the stiff westerly that was scurrying dust down Melbourne Street.

It was getting dark by the time Jack headed up the stairs and into the office. Normally it would have been cosier at home, but Vida had him in the doghouse, so it was much of a muchness. He turned on his desk lamp as raucous shouts from some GIs down the back lane heralded the encroaching dark, lined up the three photos and studied them. There was a story here; just a matter of digging it out.

Mrs C. was a real dong-stretcher, no doubt about it, and she was sure to be at the bottom of the whole caper, but he put her aside for now and looked intently at the other two photos as the gloom crowded in on the old desk and feeble lamp. There were half a dozen boys in the photo; he studied them closely, referring back to the war shot several times, before reaching into the bottom drawer and pulling out a magnifying glass. It took a while before he was sure, but the small, fair-haired kid with the arm draped around his shoulders was definitely the young Billy. The next question was: why was the photo torn . . . who was on the other half?

A bit of subterfuge might be in order. He got his camera out and fitted the new lens to it. He didn't have a stand. As a private investigator he should really have his own darkroom, but whenever visual evidence of compromising capers was required he just got it all developed by young Vern down at the chemist's. Vern was a spotty boy with the personality of floor wax, but he was no mug where a sly quid was involved, and knew his stuff: he did Jack's under-the-counter jobs after hours, when the boss had gone home, and kept copies of the juicier shots as pulling material. The arrangement suited them both.

Jack grabbed a couple of the second-hand legal volumes he kept as window dressing and was able to balance the camera over the pictures safely enough to focus right in. These lenses weren't rubbish, and he easily framed a close-up of the young boy. He took a few shots to make sure and popped down the street again, walking past the chemist's to make sure Old Man Levinson was already away to home and hearth, then straight in to his young accomplice. Vern was more than keen to whip the pictures up on the spot for an extra ten bob, and they were delivered to Jack within the hour.

"Who's he?" the young one asked with an offhand sneer, as he spread the prints on Jack's desk.

"That's for me to know and you not to worry about, sunshine," he said, handing over the dosh. "Just remember: what ya don't know can't be beaten outta ya."

That was a big enough hint of derring-do to impress the callow boy, and he winked conspiratorially as he pocketed his gains and rushed off. A light rain started to tickle the roof, and Jack buttoned up his trench coat before heading out into what was now complete darkness. An early one was called for, and he hoped the landlady would at least be dispensing some solid tucker, if not her favours. The wind grew chillier as the accompanying tempest picked up pace, and the tram arrived in a spray of dirty water. A night in was definitely the way to go, and then hit it first thing tomorrow.

"Up the hill, champ," he said to the clippie, handing over a deener.

The rain streaked the grimy windows.

4

A quick round of calls to various presbyteries revealed that St Aloysius was a boarding school just outside Toowoomba, and by lunchtime, Jack was safely ensconced in a second-class window seat at Roma Street Station. A briefcase quickly packed with fresh smalls and a cut lunch from Vida sat with a copy of Orwell's *Homage to Catalonia* on the leather beside him. He got up and poured himself a glass of water from the carafe at the end of the carriage and stood on the running platform as the train picked up speed and the suburban stations started to whiz by at a faster clip. By the time they reached open country, it was a bit chilly in the breeze so he went back to his seat and began reading, stopping every few pages to look at the land good men were fighting and dying for. The plains looked dry, even after the unseasonal showers of the last week; the grass had a silver sheen as the wind caressed it in waves that dashed against the solitary grazing beasts standing out like rocks in the ocean. It got cooler again as the train began the climb up the Range after Gatton, and the labouring of the engine filled the carriage with the trusty smell of smoke and soot as the incline grew steeper. The stopover at Spring Bluff to let a down train through gave Jack time to take in the view from the lofty, isolated siding; he took a mouthful from another glass of water then hurled the remnants onto the neat flowerbeds by the track.

The shadows were lengthening when the train arrived in Toowoomba. As Jack walked along Ruthven Street, he kept up a slow stroll, taking in the trees and gardens, until he came to the Oriental on the corner of James Street. It had come recommended by an old acquaintance and seemed to fit the bill admirably.

This'll do, he thought, as he stepped up to the bar and organised his lodgings over a welcome beer. The publican's brother had a car for hire on the sly and that was sorted out as well. The locals weren't a bad lot – a few blokes on leave, and some First War men of his own vintage – but he didn't feel like chewing over old mud 'n' slime stories, so he took his glass into the dining room and tucked into the mutton and veg put out by the owner's wife, a buxom redhead who gave him a couple of rather alluring glances as she cleared away his plates. He wasn't up for any nonsense. Admittedly it had got pretty bloody cold outside, and a willing sort to snuggle up to would have been just the ticket, but he didn't know the lie of the land. He settled for a good hot shower, and a quiet couple of largies as he boned up on his research with *The Sun Also Rises*. He had a soft spot for Ernie and his scribblings – at least the bastard had been there, and seen what he wrote about. One of his prize possessions was the *Men At War* anthology that had come out a year or so ago, put together by Hemingway and some mates. He though it should be required reading for a soldier, speaking from experience, and this opinion was shared by the powers that be. He'd heard that a shortened version was standard issue for the US Army, and he wondered whether a bit of such wisdom would do our own mob some good.

The mist was still thick when he woke at sparrow-fart – or chook-fart, more accurately, since the run next door cackled into life with the first glow of light. He shaved and dressed, then went down eager for some fresh bum nuts. He wasn't disappointed. The lady of the house was already carving bacon, and he wondered if the innkeeper had managed a few push-ups on the huge knockers that jostled in her housecoat as she laboured over the breakfast setting. He was a mug if he hadn't. Then again, familiarity often bred contempt, and the resulting jiggery-pokery kept him making a living, such as it was.

It was only a short run out on the Warwick Road to the entrance of St Aloysius. A curving drive lined with pines led to several imposing old buildings in an ornate mixture of styles you could only call Colonial Gothic.

A severe-looking clerical type came out to greet him, and they went in, leaving his driver leaning on the bonnet to light up a coffin nail as the wintry sun struggled through the clouds.

As he waited, Jack picked up a copy of *National Geographic* from the rack in the corridor outside the office. Always good for a shot of some exotic norks, in his experience, but this one had been cut to pieces – whether to protect the little dears from the sight of some cannibal's missus in the nuddy or just in the process of slopping glue about was hard to tell, but it was a waste either way. He threw it down in disgust as the door opened and a priest beckoned him in.

Recalling the rattling collection plates of his youth, Jack figured the church was always hungry for a quid, so he introduced himself as a lawyer chasing down a bequest from an old dear who had been helped out in her dotage by some young neighbour. The saintly one had moved on, but she wanted to leave something in her will for him, as well as reward the school that had turned out such a splendid chap. He offered the close-up of young Bill as the hero in question, but it rang no bells: it appeared the good Father McGarrity had only been there a few years. Another teacher was summoned with similar results, and Jack pondered the apparently unseemly rate of staff turnover in the previous decades.

Finally Jack suggested that a trawl through the class photos might produce something, and the dusty tomes were made available. He was left alone to undertake the apparently tiresome task, which was what he wanted, and he went straight to the late war years. The fact that he had a much more informative photo to work from was something he hadn't shared with the cassocked fusspots who flitted about from time to time checking on his progress, but after about a half an hour it was in the bag. The full image was staring up at him, and the names of everyone in it were on the back in neat copperplate. A hard-faced priest was on the end of the arm draped across the shoulders of the young lad on his right, and two more on his left. So far so good. And as he copied down all the names, one leapt out at him: Toby McLean.

He flipped the photo over and looked more closely at the kid in question. Sure as eggs, it had to be Crusher McLean – he even had a footy in his hand. That sugary smell you get after your noggin connects with a rock-hard paddock on a winter arvo came flooding back. Bloody hell, the front-rower with mud for blood! There he was – a bull-necked little bruiser even then, and grinning like a monkey – in the same class as our Bill. This was a turn-up!

They'd met on the field once or twice when Jack was on the wane and the Crusher in his prime, and he'd done just that: gone right through him like a late train. They'd had the odd beer after Jack hung up his boots, and Toby now coached some whippersnapper's footy nursery down Wynnum way. Jack couldn't pinch the photo; that would be too obvious, so he asked if there was any way to get a copy done in town. No need for that yet, he was told: there were a few boxes of old student copies of the annuals in a storeroom, and if the relevant one could be turned up; it was his.

The gods were smiling – unusually, in light of his religious delinquency – and a couple of the young lads dragooned into the search soon had one for him. Jack slipped them two bob each for their trouble, which they viewed as a real bonus on top of being out of their class for a bit, and was on his way quick-smart, with lots of guff about the beneficence coming the school's way from the fictitious dear departed. It had been good work, and he grinned inside on the drive to the station, admiring the multicoloured front yards of the Garden City, gleaming in the sun as it finally burnt off the low cloud that had hung about all morning. He was back in the old town by nightfall, and hurrying home with a rare bag of stone fruit he'd picked up in Toowoomba. Things were going well.

5

The cloth top of the old Austin flapped just above his head, giving him the shits as he accelerated down the mad mile. The long straight stretch was a racetrack for local mugs and hoons, who tested themselves and their conveyances on it late at night. The unforgiving gums along the roadside interrupted these shenanigans whenever judgement was wanting, inflicting severe vehicular and bodily damage with often terminal consequences. This thinned out the youth of the area without, however, discouraging the practice, hence the name by which this stretch of Wynnum Road was renowned the town over.

The amount of legwork involved in the case had started to tell on him, but a bit of arm-twisting had resulted in the various parties involved providing this old clapped-out Austin registered to the union. It wasn't a limousine by any stretch of the imagination, but it had a full tank and a glove box full of coupons, so that made up for any mechanical deficiencies. It had taken a bit of bleating and wheedling to get it, but so what? He was off shanks's pony for now, and that was the main thing.

The narrow tyres made the steering wheel judder as he sloshed down the rutted dirt track, and the odd wraith of mist hung in the dripping trees as he turned the corner in front of the pub. It was a gloomy spot, made worse by the dying of the sun somewhere up behind the low cloud.

The building had been an inn back in the dim darks before the combined efforts of town planners and commerce had sent the roads off somewhere else and initiated its slow decline. The tin roof was rusty, and the rickety verandah slumped onto the scrappy grass and muddy gravel. He pulled up next to a couple of beat-up Dodge trucks and got out. A few local brats with scabby faces clustered around the car as he stepped up onto the verandah. He smelt a strong, sweet aroma wafting around from the side. Walking past the sullen bloke staring into his draught on an old car seat at the front, he saw a 44-gallon drum with a fire ticking over underneath it and a few more scruffy little buggers in attendance.

"Muddies a bob, mister!" yelled one.

"That's a bit steep, tiger! They're a bit light this time of year."

The young feller put a stick into the bubbling broth and fished one out. It was huge.

"I might see ya for one of them in a tick," Jack said, and went inside.

There were a few candles about, either because of unpaid bills or blackouts, and they gave the whole joint a mean air. The bar was small, like an old coach-house, and the drinkers were a mangy lot. Battered hats, sleeveless shirts, and holey jumpers were the uniform, along with tweeds held up with rope. Fishermen and general roughnuts seemed to be the flavour, and the barman was as surly as they come.

"Beer's off, mate," he snarled straight up. Jack gestured to the foaming glass in front of the unshaven bloke beside him.

"What's that then, his own piss?"

The thickset man stood up quickly but unsteady; obviously well sloshed.

"What'd you say, mate?"

"I wasn't talkin' to you."

"You were fucken talkin' *about* me."

"Calm down, sport. It was a joke."

"Well I'm sayin' it wasn't funny."

"Look, settle down."

"Listen, copper."

The locals seemed sensitive about their privacy.

"I'm no copper."

"Prove it."

"Well if I was, me size ten would be firmly embedded in your arse by now, for a fucken start."

Jack was still leaning on the bar looking fairly relaxed and the primitive instincts of the drunk began to tell him that this opponent was a bit too cool. He wasn't backing off though, and he had support; Jack sensed a couple more figures gathering. He tried a different tack.

"What's with you bastards? A man comes in lookin' for an old mate, and not only will yez not serve him a rightful beer, ya wanna knock his block off. Struth, what a mob of fucken hoons. I dunno."

It didn't seem to work: the drunk shaped up, and the air was tense. He leaned over and grabbed a beer bottle as more figures started to cluster around him with grievous intent.

"Look, I've been nice so far. Now, do I have to break this on some cunt's head and cut me way outa here or what?"

"Who's ya mate?" said the barman, suddenly keen to settle things.

"Crusher McLean."

"You really a mate of Crusher's?" said the swaying drunk, all friendly now. "Ya shoulda said."

"Well how would I know who he is or where to find him if I

wasn't?"

Logic can work wonders sometimes. A beer was set in front of him immediately, and the locals backed off, grumbling, while the barman grabbed a brat by the ear and told him to go find the big feller.

"That's better, lads. Now, where is the old bastard?" Jack asked.

"With the dogs out back."

Jack took his beer and wandered out the side door after the kid, past the steaming drum of crabs and down the rutted path. About a hundred yards on he followed it through a clearing in the scrubby shitbush to an area that had all the appearances of a homemade footy oval with a running track around the perimeter.

Closer inspection revealed an iron rail running inside the low fence that surrounded the sandy track, and a cursing man pulling violently on the starter cord of an unwilling motor that graced the contraption on it. Bloody hell, Jack mused, a shonky dog track – what next? The clubhouse was a tin humpy in which a large knot of men stood arguing volubly between gulps of grog as various mangy hounds growled and whined at each other. A bloated figure detached himself at the messenger's request and shambled over.

The smell of mud and sweat came back as he remembered packing down against the man who stood before him, now a gross parody of his former finely sculpted self. They shook, and Jack took in the yellowish hue of his eyes as they exchanged pleasantries. The reddened jowls of the full-time alky creased in a smile, as the setting sun peeked through the clouds and lit up the lined features of a man gone on the piss beyond all return. They walked slowly back to the pub making small talk, and were soon cracking crab claws by the firelight and washing down the sweetest meat of all with beers aplenty.

They hadn't spoken in at least seven years and Jack was careful to make no reference to the poor state of his old footy foe. Fucken hell, he was no stranger to the neck oil, but here was a lesson in what the grog could do if it got to be the boss. After sprucing up a bit with some water from the tank, they sat back down on the hard boards of the verandah and Jack finally got around to it.

"Mate, do ya remember a bloke called Billy Callaghan?"

Toby looked at him funnily.

"Where'd that name spring up from?"

"He's topped himself."

"Shit eh?"

Crusher pushed his hat back on his head and paused to ruminate, then muttered: "That's no good, but what's it got to do with me? I haven't clapped eyes on 'im for years."

"Nothin'. But I thought you might be able to fill me in on him a bit, seein' how you was old school cobbers and such."

"Who told ya that?"

Jack handed over the school shot, and Toby angled it toward the firelight.

"Fuck me roan! Where the hell did ya get that?"

"His missus."

"Didn't know he had one!"

"Well he did. Cute too. So what can ya tell us, and who's this bloke with his arm round him, the priest?"

Toby's jaw clenched and he hung his head strangely.

"That bastard!"

"Handy with the strap, was he?"

"Oh yeah, but . . . he was special, a right dog."

"Why?"

"He was a fiddler."

"What?"

"You know . . . a molester."

"Really?"

A pause while the Crusher rubbed his chin.

"Well . . . I s'pose he's dead."

"The priest?"

"No, Bill."

"Meaning?"

Another pause.

"Well, he got up him . . . you know."

Come again?"

"He rooted him."

"Get fucked!"

"No, mate, he was foursquare up 'im! The poor little bastard."

"You knew?"

"We all knew, mate. The bastard had a go at all of us. He even pulled my toggle one time, but I thumped him when he wanted to go the whole hog. But Bill . . . shit, he served him like a fucken bull, mate. It was grim stuff."

"It's a fucken raw story, cobber. I gotta say, I've never heard the like."

"Mate, it was part of the deal in that joint. And mind you, a lotta the young blokes didn't mind gettin' their dongers tickled – willin' sheilas were pretty thin on the ground out that way. There was one old brother would even get 'em pissed as farts on communion wine and gobble 'em off. No harm really done, I'd s'pose. But that full-on caper. mate, that's a shocker. It was Delaney's form all through, and poor old Billy copped it."

"So how long did this go on for? What happened in the end?"

"Fucken nothin' much, mate! Something musta been said, though, 'cause one day Delaney just disappeared. And that was the end of it, far as I know. I think Billy went down to Sydney

Uni after high school and I never saw 'im again. A bad business, mate. I'm getting the shivers thinkin' about it, the dirty cunt."

"So this Delaney was never seen again?"

"Nah. Not there, anyway. But he's probably still about some-where. He was a bloody good coach too, for all that."

"So what about the parents?"

"Fuck, you want it all, don't ya! The old man was a chippie, ended up some big builder apparently. Look, I've had enough of this memory lane shit. Let's have another."

They stood up and went inside as the gloom slipped into night.

6

It was after nine when Jack pulled up at home. The front light revealed two figures with cloth caps and shabby coats sitting on the verandah, sucking on durries through the cupped hands of ex-cons.

Here's a go, he thought, and slid his flick-knife up his sleeve as he got out of the car.

They were standing at the top of the stairs by the time he got there, but there was no menace in their manner, so he relaxed a bit as the taller one spoke up.

"Apologies, brother, but we need that car back again."

"What, I just got the fucken thing!"

"Sorry mate, party business. We're just delivering the message. Len said you'll have it back by Tuesday. That's it, mate, sorry."

"Fuck me drunk. I was just getting used to it."

"That's what a collective's all about, brother," the small one chipped in with a grin.

Jack saw his point and flicked them the keys.

"Fair enough then. Death to the bourgeoisie, eh, cobbers."

They looked at him exasperatedly and went down to the car. He strolled inside and Vida was standing there looking grim.

"Who were those hooligans?" she demanded.

"Brothers in arms, love. Got any tucker?"

"There might be some cold cuts about," she sniffed. "It's well past tea time, as you well know. This isn't a bloody restaurant. "

As he passed her she turned: "Oh, by the way, a bloke called Sol rang for ya. He said there was a . . . *bailar*?" She checked the scrap of paper in her hand. "Yeah, that's right. Dunno what it is, but it's on tonight. Going on down by the river near Davies Park."

Old Sol was on the case for 'im – what a beaut. Jack had picked up enough Spanish in his research over the last couple of days to know *bailar* meant dancing, and he chuckled at the old bloke's tricky humour.

He grabbed a slice of corned brisket from under the cloth on the sideboard and shoved it between a couple of slices of damper as Vida grumpily poured him a black tea.

"Off out again, I presume."

"'Fraid so," he replied, and swore as he heard rain starting to drum on the roof.

He grabbed his trenchcoat from the hallstand, scalding his lips as he slurped the tea and washed the last of the sanger down. He needed it to warm him up.

It was a fair trot all the way over to that stretch of the river, and trams were thin on the ground this time of night. But it was all downhill once you got up to the crest of Dornoch Terrace, so it wasn't too bad if you didn't have to do it with a wet arse. A tram turned up when he was halfway down, but it was well after ten by the time he got there and he wondered if he'd missed it all.

A thick mist hung about the park; it was clammy but the rain had dropped off. He could hear thumping and yelling coming from inside the hall. It was more of a shed really – probably just an old footy lock-up – but cosy enough, and the wooden floor reverberated as the singing and strumming of guitars carried in the night air. A few figures wreathed in cigarette smoke stood leaning against the trees that surrounded it, and Jack slowed his pace to check out the lie of the land. A Ford sat parked on the opposite side of the road with two figures in it.

Jack crossed back over to that side and came up from behind until he was under a paperbark tree just to the rear of the vehicle. A street light glowed dully from a pole about fifty yards further up and it silhouetted the bods in the car nicely. They had to be rozzers; he waited until one of them turned to talk to the other, then felt fairly confident he knew his mark. The tall hat with the thick ribbon had confirmed his suspicions: bloody Simmo, Special Branch. He'd make Jack in a tick. It was best to brazen this out or piss off home. Old mates they might be, but Inspector James Simpson was straighter than a Roman road, and harder than calculus. He didn't appreciate his mately nature being taken advantage of, and tended to become unforgiving when he was not in the know. Jack sidled up to the offside window, which was halfway down to stop the windscreen fogging up too much.

"Got some lollies, mister?"

A surprised Jim Simpson looked up at him.

"Struth, what are you doin' here?"

"Hanky-panky, whatta ya think?"

"Shoulda known. What's the go? Some bugger got somethin' spicy on the side, eh?"

"Clickin' his castanets, by the look of it."

"Which one?"

"Not sure. Haven't been in yet. What's your game then – after a missing bullfighter?"

"Yeah right. Reds, mate. Gotta keep an eye on 'em."

"They're on our side, aren't they?"

"For the moment. But this lot run their own race, ya dunno who's who . . . anarchists, Communists, Trotskyites . . . mad buggers the lot of 'em, stab ya for tuppence. You watch yaself."

"I always do." Jack looked at his watch in mock seriousness." If I'm not out in half an hour . . ."

The inspector guffawed. "You'll be up some hot chiquita will ya?"

Jack winked. "Here's hopin'."

He thumped the top of the car and strolled over the road towards the entrance. He'd handled it well: best to front up; no point in making excuses later.

He walked across the grass to the door and handed over two bob to the old lady dressed in black who sat at the table. She handed him a ticket and motioned him inside with a nod of her hawk-like face.

Sour lookin' bugger, he thought, as he went inside. The doors facing the river were open but there was no breeze to cut through the fug of smoke from cigarettes and the cooking fire set up on the concrete apron outside. The dancers were having a break, and he checked the sallow faces of the younger men who sat around the edges of the room on benches. They seemed to be keeping their distance from the women and families at the trestle tables, who were hopping into steaming plates of food and mounds of bread.

It all looked pretty decent tucker, and Jack's guts were grumbling. He walked over and handed his ticket to a chubby señorita who promptly ladled out a plate of rice garnished with chunks of this and that.

"Pie-ella," she smiled, "Is not like at home but is good."

He took his plate, nodding thanks, and realised those were the first words anyone had said to him since he got there, as if they knew he wouldn't know the lingo. Which wouldn't take too much working out really: he was a lot bigger than most of them, and his ruddy complexion contrasted with the generally tanned faces around him.

He sat down with the plate balanced on his knee and hoed in. It was bloody good, whatever it was, and when a young girl brought him a glass of beer on a tray without being prompted, he smiled and gave her two bob, which widened her dark brown eyes considerably. She skipped off, and he looked around: a couple of the men eyed him blankly, but no one made any move to talk to him. It was a bit queer, as if they knew he was up to something but didn't care too much. A bloke in the corner was quietly strumming and tuning his guitar, then suddenly stopped as if a chill breeze had gone through the room. Jack looked over at him to see what had caused this slight disturbance in the fabric of the night.

It was her.

She stood behind the guitarist, surveying the room with an air of something between arrogance and proposition, as if she dared them to even look at her. Which was understandable. Jack had seen some beauties in his time, but she was something else. You could get Rita Hayworth and Dolores del Rio and half a dozen others rolled into one, and they wouldn't have half the blazing sexual menace and sheer desirability of this babe. No picture could do her justice. Raven hair cascaded over smooth olive shoulders, framing the biggest, reddest lips and greenest eyes imaginable. Her figure made an hourglass seem blocky, and her red dress hung from the finest set of funbags God ever breathed life into.

Jack realised his mouth was hanging open. He shut it quickly and swallowed what he'd been chewing; though she hadn't looked his way, several of the men had, and they didn't look so relaxed anymore. They weren't fools: it was now obvious what he was doing there, and they weren't impressed.

She glided around the room, followed by the eyes of every man, to the obvious disapproval of all the wives and old maids. A banner with the letters CNT was draped over a chair; she picked it up. The guitarist began to sing slowly and a hush fell over the room. The subject matter was pretty serious, judging by the bowed heads, and he figured it must be some lament for the fallen; you didn't have to be an expert to know a sad song, whatever the language. Another woman stepped up, chanted fervently, then took the banner and held it aloft. The guitarist began to strum furiously, and people joined in, clapping their hands in time and stamping on the floor. The noise began to get louder, and an unearthly wailing added to the crescendo as some of the men joined in the ululations. It was a weird sound: half-Arab, half-banshee, it seemed to Jack, and it made the hairs stand up on his neck and a lump form in his throat, even though he didn't know what the hell they were on about. It got more and more oppressive as the tempo picked up and the feet drumming on the floor became almost deafening. He drained his beer and scarpered.

Outside he paused to catch his breath, shaking. The smoke hadn't helped, but shit, he'd virtually gone into a blue funk in there, and all from a few dagoes having a bit of a singsong. This was no good; he'd been in no danger, but something had got to him. He mopped his brow and walked down to the riverbank, where he stopped for a while looking at the reflections of lights from the other side that occasionally pierced the fog, and got his measure back. Something deep in his subconscious had been disturbed by that bloody gyppo howling, and he didn't want to see what it was when its head broke the surface. Too many screaming dead men locked up down there; best keep the lid on.

Jack was heading slowly back towards the hall when he saw a figure walk out and move away towards Montague Road . . . it was her. She walked onto the footpath and stayed near the streetlights. Jack followed at a reasonable distance, staying in the darkness of the park. There was no path and he stumbled over a tree root in his pursuit. As he righted himself, he saw a figure in front of him and the gleam of a blade. A rustling to his left indicated at least one more, then a second figure appeared in front of him. They all had stilettos out and weren't looking particularly happy.

"You want the woman, mister?" said one of them in a thick accent.

"She's not bad, eh?" he said, tensing for action but still trying to take in the extent of the opposition.

"Not for you, I think," said the first one, stepping out of the gloom. A large beret hung down over his eyes; he looked dapper, but mean and dangerous. Jack angled for an advantage while he kept them talking.

"No harm in looking, fellers. Can't do much with me eyes!"

"You might lose them this night," said the one with the beret, pointing the blade at Jack's face. That was all he needed. He batted the blade aside, whipped out the .38 he had in his belt at the back and stuck it straight under the beret. At the same time he grabbed the man's shirt and twisting him round as a shield, so he couldn't get shivved by the others. The other two stopped in their tracks, taken aback by the speed at which the big feller moved.

"Righto," said Jack, "enough pleasantries. What's ya story?"

"What is yours, señor?" said one of the others. "You have come to us. We mind our own business here, make no trouble, but you . . . you are trouble."

"Fucken oath I am, so don't shit me."

The other two put their blades away, and as he glanced around he realised that the street was now empty, which was probably the aim of the whole interlude.

"You," he said to the one he had bailed up. "What's your name?"

"Juan."

"That'd be right. Well then, Don Juan, where does she live?"

"I don't know, and I tell you nothing anyway."

"I'll make ya talk," snarled Jack, screwing the gun up harder under his nose.

Juan laughed and held up his hand; the fingernails were all gone.

"The Falange couldn't, my friend, and you are an amateur."

Jack put his gun back in his belt.

"Don't bet on it, mate. Anyway, I only want to tell her something about her husband."

"That *chancho comunista!*" spat Juan, "I hope he is dead."

"Well, sport, you're right on the money. He is."

The three men all looked stunned.

"This is true?" said one.

"On my oath, mate."

"How did this happen?"

"He killed himself."

Aha! To hell for this bastard!" said the other, grinning and kissing some amulet round his neck.

"I take it you didn't like the fact he pinched one of your girls, then."

"What do you think, we are savages?" said Juan angrily "We are educated men. She was a woman of the revolution, and she made her own choice. It is none of our business. That was the old way, that we fought to destroy. Many died for this."

"Sorry fellers," said Jack, "what else *could* I think? Didn't he fight for your side though? "

"Who?"

"The husband. You obviously knew him."

"We knew him well enough. He killed many of our friends in Barcelona."

"Hang on a tick, you mean he fought for Franco?"

"No, he was a Communist!"

"Well what the fuck are you lot then?"

"We are anarchists, revolutionaries of the people. That bastard was for Stalin. The Communists betrayed the revolution."

It all clicked; lucky he'd finished Orwell's book.

"Alright," he said,. "I get it, you guys were on the same side as the POUM or whatever."

Their eyes brightened.

"Si, you know!" said one, and slapped him on the back.

Bloody hell, we're all talking like old mates here, he thought, as they walked out to where the light was better. Juan straightened himself up as more music wafted over from the hall in the distance.

Jack kept digging. "So Bill married her *before* or *after* the split, or whatever it was?"

"Before, but she is a good woman, she stayed to fight with us. Then she was captured by the Communists. They were going to shoot her, and he saved her from this, so she owes him her life and stays with him. He comes back here . . . none of us knew this, of course . . . and when she turns up here with him, the feelings are bad. Many of the women lost their husbands and sons. Now we know her story, she is forgiven by some but not by others. They have long memories. They do nothing because this is not our country and we are guests, but it was strange for her to come here. She has dishonoured her family and walks alone now. I do not know where she lives. What more is there to know? Come and drink with us."

"I gotta go," said Jack.

Juan put a firm hand under his arm.

"You don't find her this night, my friend. Come have some wine."

Jack could see the sense in that and walked back to the hall with them.

"Ya speak pretty good English, Juan," he said. "Is that how they let ya in here?"

"I speak French too," he replied. "But just as well I didn't go there. What you think, my friend?"

"I'll drink to that."

The guitar got louder as they went back into the hall.

7

Jack woke with a rough head from the wine, but it was a nice morning. He'd got quite a lot more of the drum on the lovely Mrs C, and plenty more yarns besides. Once they found out he'd killed Germans he was everyone's mate, and it had taken hours to get out of there. Not a bad bunch of blokes, really. They really believed in their cause (which you needed a lot of history to understand) and were willing to die for it. Australia could do worse than that lot.

He decided to work from home for a change and hit the phone book again. If this Delaney was on the books at any church in the state, he'd find him without getting off his arse. He hadn't greased palms to get the phone put in for nothing. Vida was in town doing the Saturday morning runaround, so he had the joint to himself. The other three boarders were either working or they'd gone back home for the weekend, so there'd be no distractions or complaints. It only took a few calls before the alphabet struck gold; Delaney himself picked up the phone at St Brendan's. Jack's mouth went dry.

"So that's Father Delaney the footy coach?"

"Yes."

There was a hint of the brogue, but it was strangely forced, as if the speaker was trying to hide it but couldn't.

"Used to be out at Toowoomba?"

Silence.

"Ya there, Father?"

"Yes."

"Didja used to be at St Aloysius?"

"A long time ago."

Jack warmed up. "Gee, I used to be one of your students."

"Really, who is this?"

"Oh it's a surprise."

"I don't like surprises."

Jack wanted to really give it to him but held off. "You'll like this one. I can't wait to see you."

"What's your name? Perhaps that'll help."

The priest's voice was trembling; that was evidence enough for Jack.

"No, you'll just have to wait."

He hung up. St Brendan's was down just past the Valley; it was all falling the right way.

Next step was the old boy network. He rang Len and asked if he had any good mates in the building unions.

"Silly fucken question!" was the expected reply.

By eleven he had the home and business addresses of Michael Callaghan Building, and a couple of early lagers in Len's office had set him up for the day nicely. He decided to go have a sniff around. Callaghan's yard was down a side street along Breakfast Creek, but there was not much activity to be seen. A young pasty-looking clerk manned the front desk, and took his role a bit too seriously for Jack's liking. He was boss of the walk that morning, without anyone of substance being about, and he wasn't what you'd call the hearty type. He was too much of a goody-goody, born to be a seat-polisher. Once it had been elicited that Callaghan himself wasn't there and wasn't coming in that day, Jack leaned over the counter and informed him that he'd just have to go out and see him at home.

"You can't do that!" said the clerk.

"How so?"

"I won't tell you where it is, or give you the number!" snapped the boy, revelling in his little bit of authority.

"I don't need it, ya twerp."

"I'll ring him before you get there," said the officious one, and he wasn't being helpful.

Jack turned on his best menacing tone and stared right at the lad from as close as he could get. "You do what ya want, young feller, but get in my way and I'll come back here and shove some of this hardwood so far up ya date, ya'll have splinters in ya teeth."

The young one's spectacles misted up and he sat down.

"He won't be there, mister," he said, obviously chastened.

"Why not?"

"He's inspecting a job out at Ipswich, he'll be back in the yard on Monday."

"That's more like it, sonny. Good manners go a long way."

Jack chuckled as he went back down the wooden stairs. He'd been a bit rough on the young cove, but fuck 'im, life's tough. It'd help him grow up right.

What to do now? Plenty of time to have an arvo off and catch a film or something. It was only half a dozen stops back to the Valley. These buggers would all keep. No one was going anywhere; he was chasing a dead man.

8

The tram sat silently outside the Imperial as the drivers changed shifts, and he could hear a race-caller's nasal drone wafting through the air from the pub radio. He got off and strolled inside. As he sat in the corner with the form guide left behind by someone who'd either quit ahead or cut and run, he decided it might be time to spend the arvo creatively. A phone call or two from the booth in the lounge got him through to an old mate who used to be an ambo, and from there he had the name of a connection at the morgue. It would be twenty quid for a look at the autopsy report, and he could do it that day without moving a muscle. It was just a matter of waiting where he was until the right feller strolled in and left it on his table while he went for a piss. This was more like it: bugger the shoe leather routine!

But nothing is as easy as it sounds: the joker from the morgue arrived soon enough, but he was empty handed, and looked a bit spooked.

"Mate, where's the file?" Jack said.

"Shit, mate, you don't want much!" was the reply.

"That's right, so where is it?"

"Bugger that, sport. It's been took!"

"By who?"

"Some ranker from the cops. O' Reilly, I think. He's got the bastard and I can't get within cooee of the bloody thing."

"Is that right?" Jack mused, rubbing his chin. "So can you give us an idea of when it might come back into your grasp, or what?"

"Mate, fucken fuck that for a game of soldiers. I copped billyo for even askin' about it. You're bloody lucky I showed up at all, so I better cop something for me trouble, even if it is bad news."

"Look, I appreciate the effort and all that, but what you're givin' me isn't worth a cuntful of cold water. If you want some of the folding, I need more."

"Are you deaf, sport? I told ya, I can't get near it at any price, and I reckon I done you a big favour by letting ya know the lie of the land. I coulda dropped ya in it."

"Yeah, righto, settle down. Here's a fiver for your trouble."

"Keep it comin', mate. We're not at the fucken Salvos here."

"Mate, I need more."

"Look, this is the prick stretched his neck, isn't it? Well, the only thing I remember out of the ordinary was that he had olive oil on his wrists and forehead."

"Fucken run that by me again – olive oil?"

"Yep, not a lot, but it was there. Don't sheilas use it on their skin or something? Maybe he was a poo man."

"Mate, if you'd seen his piece you wouldn't be sayin' that."

"Well, who knows why but it was there."

"Dunno what that means, if anything . . . but alright, how's ten then?"

"Half a loaf I s'pose. I gotta get back or I'll be in the pudden."

He pocketed the note and took off furtively. Jack sat back and drained his beer; the bloke had been not much help after all. But one thing was plain to see: he hadn't put on a show just to squeeze a few more bob, he'd been scared. You know these things when you've been that way yourself. And that only meant one thing: the death was suspicious, and people were going to some lengths to make it appear the opposite.

Time to go to church.

9

The winter sun shone weakly through some plane trees as the lengthening shadows lined up with the stone steps in front of St Brendan's. He walked inside and smelled the quaint, distant pong of frankincense and candle wax. It was confession time, and a line of various bods sat in one of the pews opposite the booth and shuffled along as one more sinner pushed the curtain aside to go back to the last row, kneel down, and do the requisite number of Hail Marys and so forth.

Great system, he thought. Do whatever takes ya fancy, then cough up to the priest, and all you have to do is mumble a few old rhymes and piss off out the door scot-free, ready to do it all again. It explained a lot.

He sat in the quiet, accentuated as it was by the reverent efforts of everyone else whispering or hushing one another.

There was a flurry of curtains and he saw the priest pop out the back into the nave, probably heading off for a piss break. It was definitely Delaney, the years hadn't changed him that much. But then, you're only as old as the boy ya feel, as they say. Jack got up and joined the queue. His eyes roved around the church as he waited. The seating was hard but of a very high quality: red cedar for sure, finely polished by the bums of the faithful.

All the fittings were also of dark wood, oak and mahogany, and he pondered the relationship between colour and mood. All places of power seemed dark and solemn: there wasn't much shiny pine in a courtroom, either.

His turn came in about half an hour. It was time for a bit of tin rattling: he remembered the first bit: "Bless me, Father, for I have sinned."

"Yes, my son?"

"You've never had one, pal, unless boys give birth."

The prayer book hit the floor, and the wooden window slid back hard.

"What did you say? Who are you?"

"One of your old pupils, Father."

The distorted, bug-eyed face of the priest pressed up against the grille.

"How dare you! Get out of here!"

"Righto, see ya outside and we'll have this out."

He got up smiling and went around the back as the priest pushed past him and opened the door to the sacristy. It was a heavy old oak thing. and it slammed solidly behind him as the man in black whirled around, eyes blazing.

"Now, who are you?"

"Toby McLean."

"Don't lie to me!"

"Why? Will I have to say some penance?"

"Listen, you. I know you aren't McLean!"

"How so? You would only ever have looked at the top of his head, wouldn't ya?"

The priest was nearly apoplectic. "I never touched him."

"How unusual!"

"I'll call the police!" foamed the agitated cleric.

"Yeah let's . . . We can explain everything, that'll be fun!"

Delaney drew himself up to his full height and went tough. "You're the one who phoned, aren't ya? Well, I'm not to be fooled with, mate. Out with it – what do you want? Is it money?"

That was more like it, no denials now.

"No, I want to know about a bloke called Callaghan. Another old boy of yours, wasn't he? And we know you fucked him . . . It's how recently that interests me."

Delaney's face went grey. "What do you mean?"

"You were there when they cut him down, weren't ya?"

"How do you know that?"

"Listen, you fucken old turd, I know a lot more than you think, but not quite enough. Yet . . ."

Delaney looked from side to side and fidgeted, all bluster long gone. "He was dead when I got there, I couldn't help that."

"Well that's all a bit bloody coincidental for my money, feller."

"I was the family priest!"

"Fucken bullshit! You hadn't seen him for years, and he was a Communist to boot."

"Not at the end he wasn't!"

"How so?"

"He'd come back to the Church."

"What? Through your good offices? You of all people? That's too much, I don't believe a fucken word of it."

"Believe what you like, there it is. They all come back in the end. The Lord works in mysterious ways."

Jack had only ever heard that said as a joke, so he was unsure of his ground now, and stood shaking his head. "That's for fucken sure. So when did this happen?"

"In the war, I suppose. There are no atheists in foxholes you know."

That sparked Jack back up again. "Is that right? And you'd

know, would ya? The only holes you've been in are hairless ones, you fucken germ. Listen here, I'm not happy with any of this, it's all a bit too fucken neat. You'll hear from me again, sport. Sooner or later the truth will out, mate, and you better hope it makes you look good."

"I fear nothing," intoned the priest righteously. "The Lord watches over his own."

"I thought that was the devil," Jack grunted. He opened the door and strolled back through the church and out into the gathering gloom of the winter evening. As he passed the second from last pew, he saw a figure kneeling in prayer, a mantilla covering her head. Something made him slow down and look without meeting her eye. He nearly gasped out loud. It was her, Mrs Callaghan in the flesh, and what flesh it was, even under the black dress, shawl and veil. He kept walking as his mind raced. What was going on? This was getting ridiculous.

He trotted down the steps and across the road into a mean, threadbare little park with a rusty metal bench, and sat with his arse perched on the cold steel. He wasn't going anywhere till she did. He wished he had his overcoat.

It was nearly eight o'clock before the dark figure stepped daintily out and began walking towards Ann Street. He kept about fifty yards behind her, then crossed the main road a bit further up from where she waited at the tram stop. She boarded the first one that came by and sat in the front compartment, so he was easily able to jump on board as it pulled away and head down the back where he could keep an eye on things. The streets were not yet rowdy, but the lights that were permitted were on, and it would be a lively Saturday night in the old town once the Yanks started coming in from their camps.

She stayed on right through town and across the bridge, then got off on Boundary Street, about four stops past Jack's office. This is handy, he thought, staying on the opposite side of the street from the lone figure walking quickly in the gathering night. She soon turned down a side street toward the river, continuing until she came to an old block of timber flats that poked out of the side of the hill on rickety stumps. As he stood in the shadows of a tree, she went down the verandah to the end door and knocked. A scruffy male figure opened the door, looked around furtively, and ushered her inside.

10

The office was just as chilly as outside, so he got his coat from the rack and put it on before gathering some official-looking forms and folders into a small briefcase. It was only another ten minutes and he was knocking on the door of the rundown flat, his hat in his hand.

The unshaven and surly young man who opened the door wasn't pleased to see him, and had that special arrogance the mixture of youth and dissipation brings.

"Whattya want, mate?"

"Good evening, I'm wondering if you know much about life insurance."

His foot shoved in the door stopped it being slammed shut in his face, and he kept up the pretence. "I know a lot of people haven't given it much thought, but in today's trying times . . ."

The door opened up again.

"Take ya fucking foot out of the door or I'll iron you out!" the untidy one spat as he opened it wider, giving Jack a good opportunity to case the joint. It was as untidy in décor as the tenant was in dress, but one detail stuck out: army boots behind a mop and bucket in the hallway. Jack kept at it.

"So I can't interest you in an overview of the generous provisions of our plan?"

"Listen, mate, the only thing I'm interested in is seeing you get off my bloody doorstep and piss off back to wherever ya sprang from with ya bullshit, alright?"

A figure came out into the hallway to see what was happening. "Who is it, Terry?"

"Mind your own fucken business, moll," was the reply as she came further into view, wrapped in a silk robe that looked right out of place in the dingy surroundings. Jack only got a glimpse, but it was enough for him to see the huge shiner and the split in her bottom lip that was just starting to heal.

He said nothing, and stepped slowly backwards so Terence could slam the door. Just as he did so, he sensed a presence behind him and turned to see one of the most massive women he'd ever encountered, glowering at him with a broom in her hand. She wasn't fat exactly, just bloody big, a foot taller and wider than him at his best. The huge arms that hung out of the dress would have done a wharfie proud; so would her tattoos. It was frightening.

"Who are you, ya bastard?" she hissed through cracked hairy lips protruding from the ugliest visage he'd seen in years.

"Insurance," he replied, smiling weakly.

"You'll need plenty if you ever set foot here again, feller. Now piss off."

Shit, he thought, I'm backing out of this one for now.

"Good night," he said as got to the footpath.

'It'll be good when you're gorn," she snarled. "So keep fucken walkin' if ya know what's good for ya."

Jack walked slowly back to the office, where he ruminated for a while before heading home on the last tram. Vida was still up.

"You know most of the old birds in your game round here,

don't ya, Vi?" he asked, after a cup of tea had been served up.

"Most of 'em. Why?"

"Big ugly sheila runs a joint just off Montague Road, run-down sorta block?"

"Bloody hell! Crossed her, have ya? Struth, ya better watch it. She'll bite ya leg off."

"Fairly aggressive bugger, for sure. What's the story?"

"Val Cox is her name, and there's that many stories . . . where do ya start?"

"That wouldn't be Benny Cox's widow, would it?"

"Exactly, and she was worse than him."

The late Benny Cox was a classic standover man who'd flourished during the Thirties preying on small-time crims and bookies and the like. Jack had arrested him once for drunk driving and possession of a firearm, but Benny had been connected enough to walk away from it without much of a penalty and no time inside. Their paths had never crossed again, but Benny thought he was destined for higher things, and extended his attention to a visiting bookie from Melbourne who was up for the Doomben Cup. The visitor viewed it as rather discourteous to be pistol-whipped and relieved of a couple of grand during his stay, and apparently made his displeasure known to some of his associates when he got home. Rumour had it that a certain South Melbourne waterfront enforcer arrived on a train the very next week, and soon thereafter Bigshot Benny was found floating off Cribb Island, his throat cut from ear to ear and the razor jammed up his arse. His widow had apparently come down a peg or two since then, but according to Vida she was still engaged in sly grog and other infractions of the legal code, while running the rental premises she'd bought with what remained of Benny's stash.

"Trust me, Jack," Vida said. "Steer clear."

"Have you got any solid mail or is it all scuttlebutt?"

"I dunno, love, I mind me manners about that stuff. Better not to know. But it's a pretty unsavoury sort of place, going by the tenants . . . although Val's been pretty quiet since the son went off."

"What? There was a son?"

"Yep, a chip off the old block apparently. Got done for stealing cars and god knows what else, and took the King's shilling instead of a jail term. He's up in New Guinea somewhere being a hero, we're told."

"Is that so? What was his name, do you know?"

"Denny? Teddy, maybe? Can't really remember. Why?"

"Oh nothing. Anyway, love, off to bed for me. I've got an early one."

"Is that it?" she said, somewhat affronted. "Don't feel like company?"

"Not tonight love, I'm knackered," he lied, as his brain kept replaying pictures of the bruised face of Mrs Callaghan and his imagined healing kisses.

He was becoming besotted. And that made for bad judgement.

11

It was fairly pelting down as the tram trundled over Breakfast Creek and headed out towards Ascot. The grey hulks of warships tied up on the Bulimba reach loomed through the rain as he got to Hamilton; he alighted a couple of stops past Breakfast Creek and started climbing the steep hill to the mansions that sat above.

The views would have been spectacular on a clear day, but it was still a pretty spot whatever the weather. Callaghan's residence was set back but still dominated the street; this was the big end of town alright, and his was a big house in it.

The gravel drive was a bit muddy as he got close to the entrance, so he stopped and wiped his shoes on the grass before climbing the steps to the huge front door. It had one of those pull-ropes, like some toff's joint in a film, and it worked some sort of bullhorn out the back, which brought a manservant along in short order.

"Good afternoon. I'm here to see Mr Callaghan."

"Sir has an appointment?"

"Not exactly. It's a family matter."

"How so?"

"Is it your place to ask, mate?"

That caught him up. He looked Jack up and down as you

would a bad painting, then stepped back and ushered him into a sitting room.

"Wait here, sir."

It was pretty plush, and Jack took a bit of a squiz at the framed photos lined up in serried rows on every possible surface, with dozens more hanging from the walls. Callaghan got on well with the clergy, by the look of things; every second shot was of him with a bishop or whatever, shaking hands outside a building. Certain similarities in style meant that you'd have to be pretty thick not to work out that he built churches and schools and virtually anything with four walls that the local god-botherers required. An exclusive contract and, going by the surroundings, most advantageous to the pocket.

The squeak of shoe leather on the polished floor made him turn around, and a florid faced man of fair size stood there in the doorway, Jack put down the photo he was perusing and walked over with his hand out. Nothing was proffered in reply.

"And you are?"

"Jack Munro."

"And your business?"

"Your son."

Callaghan's eyes lit up, but his brow darkened. "I have no son."

"Well, not now, I know, but . . ."

"Not for many years, Mr Munro. He is never spoken of in this house. Good day to you."

"Wait a minute."

"Why should I? Nothing you have to say could possibly be of interest to me."

"That's a bit harsh, isn't it, mate? He's only been dead a week or so. You do know that?"

"My son died a long time ago."

"Well, no. He didn't."

"He did for us. And what damned business is it of yours any-way?"

"Well, I'm investigating his death, actually."

"Oh really? You're not the police, so who are you?"

"I'm a private agent."

"Hired by whom?"

"Some friends of his."

"Those church-burning vermin that stole his soul, no doubt. I'll have no godless bolsheviks in my house. Get out!"

"Listen, sport. I don't give a stuff who believes what, or who pays me. All I know is that his death wasn't a plain suicide."

"I don't care, do you understand? Now get out of my house!"

This was going nowhere. Jack walked toward the door, and as he passed the fuming businessman he turned: "He went back you know."

"To what."

"The church."

"Rubbish."

"Well, why was there a priest there?"

"Where?"

"At the flat."

"There wasn't."

"That's not what he says."

"Who?"

"The priest, a Father Delaney. Heard of him?"

"No. It still means nothing to me."

"Now, look."

"No, you look. I have no interest in hearing any details of the death of that man. Now go before I have you thrown out."

Jack stopped. "I thought your religion was all about forgive-ness."

"There are some things beyond forgiveness, Mr Munro. I find it hard to believe that the Saviour himself could forgive Tarém. There must be a special part of hell reserved for those who were there."

"Where?"

"A place called Tarém. Your masters will know it well."

With that Callaghan stomped down the hall and out of sight. Jack turned and walked out through the door the butler grimly held open. He was doing up his coat before heading off into the drizzle when a long black Humber pulled in and a portly figure in purple robes got out under an umbrella the chauffeur held over his head. One more bishop for the picture gallery, no doubt. Jack walked off. Tarém, eh? Never heard of it.

The rain was intermittent as he walked down the steep street, and he stood under a tree at the tram stop to stay dry. It was Sunday, so there might not be a tram for quite a while. He'd been waiting about twenty minutes when a black sedan came around the corner and pulled up right in front of him.

It was Inspector O'Reilly and his sidekick Mulvaney, a mono-browed bruiser of the old-fashioned stamp who let his boots do the talking in most situations. They looked glum. O'Reilly opened the back door, and Jack got in.

It was warmer inside the car than out, but that didn't make him comfortable. Jack went way back with this bastard, and the memories were all bad. The last time they had crossed paths, when Jack was still on the force, it had been a rum do all round.

O'Reilly didn't mince words.

"What are you doing, you Red bastard? I always knew you were no good! Who the fuck do you think you are, sticking your nose into the affairs of the Church?"

Jack wasn't in any mood for pontification from the red-haired cop with the beak nose.

"Jesus Christ, go and get fucked, you spud-munching prick. And mind your own fucken business!"

"Stop blaspheming back there!" shouted Mulvaney from the driver's seat.

"Go piss on a post," Jack replied, flicking the burly one's ear and making him turn around, snorting with rage.

The Inspector spoke up quickly to defuse things. "It *is* my business when a bent ex-copper . . ."

"Bent? That's fucken rich! There was at least two thousand quid on that Murphy feller when I picked 'im up and only half that turned in as evidence. You and ya dog-faced mate here were all over me."

O'Reilly held the twitching Mulvaney back in his seat.

"You got your slice."

On the night in question, O'Reilly and his side-kick had pulled him out of the station-room and frogmarched him downstairs, where they conveniently found a hundred quid in a rolled-up newspaper in Jack's locker. Jack had never seen it before, but they'd planted it for a reason. He was given a choice: take it and shut up, or be charged with stealing evidence and corruption. They had him cold and he wore it . . . Mind you, it didn't go astray with the wife's psychiatrist's bills, but he'd crossed over, even if under duress. It didn't sit well. Murphy, the bankrobber, never disputed the evidence and got six months, which seemed a bit light, but Jack had not been called to the stand so it wasn't down to him either way.

"What choice did I have?"

"None, Sunny Jim, just like now. You stay away from Delaney and Callaghan, or you'll find yourself in a spot of serious bother."

"Is that right?"

"You can bet your teeth on it."

Jack shook his head. "Your gall astounds me, mate. You're as crooked as a dog's hind leg and ya fucken lecture me like some do-gooder, while your pocket's been well and truly lined since god knows when."

"I never kept that money," replied the tall Irishman.

"Oh yeah?" Jack scoffed. "Where'd it disappear to, then?"

"It went to a good cause, that's all you need to know."

The emphasis he put on the word *cause* sounded like a slip-up, and Jack filed it away as he got out into the drizzle. O'Reilly tipped his hat and said, "Top of the morning to ya. Go carefully now," then slammed the door as Mulvaney gunned the engine and raced away, spraying Jack's tweeds with dirty water from the large puddle in the gutter.

This was getting like a whirlpool, and Jack began to think it might be better to just ride it around, like the bloke in the Poe story, rather than see what was at the bottom. Then again, why not take a look. Life is short.

Len was still in his office when he got there, and Jack bowled him a googly.

'Where's Tarém, mate?"

"What sort of silly fucken name's that? What is it?"

"Dunno. Not round here for a start. Overseas somewhere, I'd s'pose."

"Hang on, I'll just pull that atlas out of me arse where I left it overnight . . . How the fuck would I know?"

"Well our dead mate's old man reckons you lot know all about it."

"Yeah? Well, fuck him! 'Cause I don't."

"Can ya get hold of that four-eyed dill for me?"

"Why?"

"'Cause he might know where this joint is. If it's got a bearing on all this bullshit, I want the drum, so knock him up for us."

"Righto. I'll ring their office if it'll shut your whingeing up."

Clancy and one of his offsiders appeared about an hour later, after a couple of beers had gone down with the setting sun, or what little of it got a look-in through the cloud. After Jack told them that Bill's death looked like it had a bit more to it than first appeared, they were happy as Larry: it was what they wanted to hear anyway, so it was lucky he wasn't making it up. But he told them straight up he needed to know a lot more from their side as well. Bill and his dodgy past was a good place to start.

"Alright, mate. Now, what and where is Tarém."

"Who told you about it?"

"Someone connected with the death of your good mate, so out with it."

"Very well. Tarém is a village between the Sierra de Caballs—"

"—the serrated what?"

"Sierra means mountains."

"Alright. And where are they?"

"A hundred miles or so west of Barcelona."

"I get the picture. Go on."

"Bill Callaghan was leading a patrol near there, near the end of July in '38, when they passed a small seminary."

"A what?"

"Seminary . . . a school, a college for young brothers."

"Whose brothers?"

"No, Christian brothers."

"Oh yeah, the apprentice priests."

"If you like. That'll do. Anyway, they came under fire from the building and three of Bill's men were killed."

"Wait a sec, was this the International Brigades, or your mob?"

"He was attached to a Republican battalion. He was never in the Brigades."

"Bit unusual, wasn't it?"

"The Party made the decisions, and besides, the Brigades were withdrawn in '38."

"Bill didn't wanna come home, eh?"

"He saw it as a lifelong struggle."

"S'pose so. Anyway, then what."

"Well they stormed the building and captured everybody. Some brothers, a few novitiates, a couple of priests, some servants."

"I think I know where this is going."

"Things happen in the heat of war."

"Some of them got the chop, I'll bet."

"All of them."

"The whole lot?"

"Yes, the young ones as well. Some were only twelve or thirteen."

"Shit eh? That's rough stuff."

"Undoubtedly. Plenty of priests were shot but the rule was generally that you checked for a bruise on their shoulder . . . to see if they had actually fired a weapon. But not this time. Bill must have lost his mind for a while."

"So how many died."

"Nearly forty, all told."

Jack pushed his hat back and crossed his arms.

"In cold blood? That's a good day's work, alright."

"It was a bit of a propaganda disaster for a while, but as things got worse it was sort of forgotten. Although the Nationalists made sure that anyone from that unit who was captured later was shot immediately. Which is a bit of a laugh – those bastards did things just as bad or worse . . . the Moroccans, fucking

Jesus! The things they did to our women. They were savages!"

"Your women, eh? You seem pretty clued up on this, Clancy . . . You weren't there yourself by any chance?"

"I was in Perpignan, over the border, trying to stay ahead of the French police and smuggle a few guns. But I heard enough about it at the time. A bad business, but there you go."

"Right. Well, I dunno what bearing it's got on what happened to Bill, but I know one thing for sure."

"And that is?"

"Why he did it."

12

It was only a fifteen-minute stroll back over to the church, and he opened the door quietly without even noticing that he had. The church was empty except for a lone figure kneeling in the second row from the back, as before. She had it bad, alright. She didn't look up as he sat down on the other side of the aisle. It was cold in there; he couldn't imagine how her knees must be feeling if she'd been on them for any length of time. He wanted to approach her but wasn't too sure about how; it was like being a giddy teenager. The minutes passed and then a door softly opened and the black clad figure of Delaney seemed to glide down to the end of his pew, then nodded towards the door.

Once outside the priest started in hard. "You don't give up, do you?"

"Nope, the more I learn about this the less I like it."

"Really?"

"Yes. For instance: how come you turn up at the scene of the crime before the cops, but the cove had no phone, and he was dead anyway, so he couldn't have called you even if he had?"

"He called from a phone box."

"Fuck off!" Jack snorted. "Are you trying to tell me he just wanders down the road, drops in his pennies and says: 'Oh, can you drop round when you have a minute, Father? I'm just about to top meself. I'll be gorn when you get here!' And you just go: 'See you soon, there's a good chap'."

"Of course not. But he did sound troubled, which is why I came straight over."

"Troubled? That's a fucken understatement. And he gave you no clue so you could try and talk 'im out of it."

"None at all. What can I tell you? That's what happened. He must have fallen further into despair in the time it took me to get there."

"If you think I'll swallow that, you're a bigger fool then I thought. This is all a smokescreen. You either know who killed him or you did it yourself, how's that for a theory?"

The priest blanched. "Don't be ridiculous. I'm a man of God!"

"God must be hard up if he needs the likes of you on board, mate. Anyway, I'm gunna go back in there and soak up the atmosphere, while you think about telling me what really happened."

He turned and went back into the church, followed by Delaney, who hurried the length of the building before vanishing into its nether regions. The praying figure hadn't moved. Jack sat back down and waited.

He pulled out his good old railway watch. Over an hour had passed, and it had become dark outside, and still she fingered the rosary and mumbled under her breath. It was giving him the willies. There would be no surprises about her destination when she finally left here, so he decided to get an early mark. He'd go back to the office, spruce up, have a bite, and then pay another visit to the flat and stir the possum.

The wind was up, rustling leaves along the deserted street as he headed back towards the main road. As he passed the end of an alley, he thought he saw something moving, and figured it was probably a cat. It wasn't.

Two burly figures leapt out at him and one connected with a crash tackle, catching him completely off balance and knocking him to the deck, where the other one started tap-dancing on him with plenty of vim. As he thrashed around on the bitumen, trying to avoid the flying boots, he accidentally grabbed the hubcap of a car parked beside the footpath, and it came away in his hands. This changed things: it had an inch or so lip and his hand fitted neatly inside the curve, so he could get a serious grip on it. Down but not out, he thought, as he swivelled around on his back and slammed the edge into the shin of the nearest assailant, who yelled and staggered forward, tripping over Jack and interfering with the kicking of his mate. A man can be dangerous working low, and before the man could get up, Jack let fly with a left straight into the balls of the one doing the kicking, then swung the hubcap like an axe straight into the back of his skull as he went down. The other one was clutching his shin and trying to get to his feet when Jack chopped him in the face with a great swing like a discus thrower, knocking him back over the mudguard of the car. Jack drove the hubcap into his face again, and started going berko.

He was back in the mud, going hammer and tongs with the fucken Prussians again. It haunted him: the Hun cavalry had got behind them one time after they'd pushed out too far without support, and Jack went hand-to-hand with one of them who he'd pulled off his horse after it stumbled in a shell-hole. They'd been strangling each other as best they could until Jack got the Jerry's helmet off and set to crowning him with it. Somehow he managed to drive the Pickelhaube right into the German's eye-socket. That did the trick, but when he decided to souvenir the helmet, the eyeball goo that came back out stuck to his tunic for ages – it put him off oysters for life.

The red mist cleared a bit and Jack realised he'd better stop before he killed this prick. He dropped the hubcap and swung the now limp figure face down over the bonnet, reefed his arm up behind his back, and opened up the questioning,

"Who the fuck are yez, and what's ya story."

"Fuck off!" said the other.

Jack grabbed his hair and slammed his dial into the metal.

"Talk fast, cunt, or I'll keep goin'."

"Alright, alright! Settle down!"

"Settle down? Fuck that! Ya jump a man, kick him when he's down, and you want *me* to settle?"

"It's nothin' personal!"

"It'll feel personal when I tear off this arm and shove it up ya fucken arse, mate. Now talk!"

"Righto! The coach told us to dust ya up a bit."

"The coach? Of what?"

"The team."

"What fucken team?"

"The Shamrocks. The reserves!"

I'm an Easts man, thought Jack, puzzled.

"What did I ever do to you blokes?"

"You're a Red!"

"No I'm not. But anyway, go on."

"Well the coach said you were a commo agitator making trouble in the parish."

"And the coach's name would be?"

"Father Delaney."

It was starting to make sense. Fucken rockchoppers stuck together, you couldn't play for the Shillelaghs (as they were known) without having attended a Catholic school. As his blood cooled, Jack took a good look at his two attackers. The one on the ground started to come to, and Jack stomped on his ear, driving his head back into the gutter.

"Fuck, sport, ease up!" said the other. "We got training Tuesday night."

"It'll toughen 'im up in the ruck, mate," Jack replied, as he realised that these were only youngsters. Big ones, to be sure, but fucken babies really. He'd been killing men at their age, but it wasn't their fault. Still, lessons must be learnt . . .

He swung the one he still held onto the next parked car and kneed him fair in the balls, then stood over the two prostrate forms.

"You go back and tell that poofter priest of yours I'm not gunna be put off by a coupla nongs like you two. I'm gunna find out what the score is, and he's gunna tell me. I've got no respect for him or his cloth, and I'll flog him like a naughty dog if I have to. And while you're at it, tell 'im this: don't send boys to do men's work. Alright?"

Mumbled assent came from the limp figures below. Jack straightened his tie and set off to get a beer somewhere. This was getting murkier by the minute.

13

Win or lose, the morning after a good blue is always a bastard, he thought, and worse the older you got. Various muscles got pulled, bones bruised and so forth, and you just can't back up like twenty years ago. Mind you, the same thing applied to bed and bottle . . . but you kept going. His eyes glanced towards the bottom drawer of the old pine dresser; there was a tin in there with a pipe and some nice tar that would take the day away if he felt so inclined.

He didn't have long to think about it. A loud thump was followed by the door springing open. Two suited figures loomed over the bed as he struggled to sit up. He was about to go for the .38 in the bedside drawer when his gaze cleared and he saw it was Inspector Simpson and his offsider Jenkins.

"Fuck, who needs an alarm clock! Whattya you dills want?"

"Some straight talking from you."

"Why, what's the go?"

"Well for a start, why are ya hangin' round a church, beltin' up young lads so they can't run the pill around for their colours?"

"I found religion."

"Always the boofhead . . . Rightio, if that's the way you want to play, let's go down the station."

The thought of sitting in a hardback chair with these mugs badgering him didn't appeal. "Leave off, will ya? Bloody hell!"

Vida's head appeared round the doorframe. "Everything alright, gents? Oh, hello Jim!"

"Mornin', Vi. Couldn't rustle up some cuppas, could ya?"

"Of course!"

Jack had sat up and pulled on his strides by now, and was leaning back against the headboard.

"Alright, then. So you guys think it's dodgy too, eh?"

"What is?"

"The hanging."

"What hanging?"

"Callaghan."

"Who's he?"

"Let's back up," said Jack. "You tell me why you're down at the chapel first."

"No, you first."

"Fucken come on, where are we? The schoolyard? You came here."

"So what, start talkin'."

"Fuck off. You first."

"No, you first."

"We'll toss for it."

"Fair enough."

Jack got two bob out of the ashtray and up it went: he won. Simpson sat down on the only chair in the room and left his mate leaning up against the wall looking officious. He took his hat off and threw it on the bed.

"This Delaney . . . Seen his brother at all?"

"Didn't know he had one."

"Well he has, and you've met him."

"Not that I remember."

"Well that's 'cause he was called Murphy at the time."

"Let me guess: a bank robber?"

"Exactly. His real name is Declan Delaney, IRA Sergeant at Arms, or so the Poms informed me when they checked his prints on a social visit. Wanted for the murder of several people in Belfast and surrounds, and numerous robberies and general bad behaviour besides. Not a nice bloke."

"There's a war on, isn't there? It's a fucken long way to come over some domestic barney."

"Well, not as it turns out! His prints were found again in Sydney last week, after some revolvers and a dozen grenades were filched from a truck that got bailed up near Holsworthy. These bastards are pulling all sorts of sabotage and what have you back in the old country, helping Jerry agents and such, so who knows what the prick might try here? Seeing as his brother Brian is the parish priest down at St Brendan's, we thought it wise to keep an eye on things, in case he turned up back here looking for a handout or hidey-hole. And what do you know? There's this big clown called Munro hangin' round like a fart in a jar for no reason I can fathom, and getting in the way. So out with it. What's the connection?"

Jack gave him as much of the drum as he could, leaving out the wife and deserter aspect of it and playing up the Communist angle. Simpson liked to think nothing got by him on his patch, so anything involving Commos was music to his ears. They had their cuppa, and just as they were winding up Jack dropped one more in the pond for good luck:

"Mate, why would a dead man have olive oil on him?"

"Search me," said Simmo.

"Extreme unction!" piped up Jenkins, who'd been quietly taking it all in.

"What's that?" said Jack.

"Last rites. The priest puts holy oil on the wrists and fore-head and so on. They use olive oil that's blessed, or some shit."

"Are you a Catholic on the sly, mate?" said Simmo.

"No but the wife is, or was. It's some ceremony they do to send the soul to heaven or something."

"But having necked himself, wouldn't this bloke be heading for the hot spot?" Jack mused.

"I s'pose . . . I dunno. Don't they bury suicides outside holy ground or whatever they call it."

Jack sat up, suddenly enlightened: "That's right! You couldn't give a suicide the last rites. It's against their law, I'm sure of it. So why the fuck would he do it if he wasn't supposed to?"

Simpson chuckled. "Who knows . . . But mate, so far your evidence isn't worth two knobs of goatshit. You can keep running in circles with this one as long as they pay ya to, for all I care, but if you stumble over any Paddies in the process, don't forget this Delaney's armed and dangerous, as they say, so no heroics."

"Who, me? I haven't got any medals."

Both cops laughed and headed out, doffing their hats to Vi on the way out.

This was getting rugged. He needed a break. A gentle puff might be the go. As he stared across the room, he felt the pull of the old first-aid tin full of goodies. But he decided against it. He needed his edge at this point, and dreams will always keep.

14

Jack caught the tram back to the office about dark and got off just as a city-bound tram passed. Mrs C was on it. She didn't see him, because the lights were on inside and he was in the gloom, but she probably wouldn't have known him from the brief glimpse the night before. She was obviously off back to the kneeling position again.

The consumption of several beers after lunch had livened him up, and a bit of piss and vinegar was brewing. He decided to stroll over and see how young Terence was getting on.

He walked quietly past the door of the front flat, which Vi had told him was Mrs Cox's lair, and down to the door at the end of the verandah, He knocked once and it flew open.

"Fuck! Not you again!" the youth sneered.

Head-butting is a tricky business, especially where height is an issue: come in at the wrong angle and you just crack noggins, which can be as bad on the giver as the taker. Fortunately Terry was looking up at him in a posture of defiance, presenting the nose and other softer parts exactly as prescribed. Jack drove his head forward and down crunching the younger man's face into a bloodied mess as he bounced backwards off the walls of the hallway before sprawling onto the kitchen lino. Jack followed up with a good kick to the ribs. The prone figure doubled up, winded, which muted the squealing coming from the mashed nose and lips.

"Righto, toughshit." Jack squatted beside him. "I think you're a fucking malingerer who's gone over the fence, and a wife-beater into the bargain. I don't approve of pricks like you."

He didn't get the next bit out. The rolling pin caught him on the side of the head and sent him crashing sidewards into a chair, which collapsed as the towering figure in a filthy apron swung the weapon back to try and brain him with the next blow. His head was spinning and he couldn't get up, but he slid out of the way as the rampaging giant lashed out again, screeching like a harpy: " I'll kill you, you fucken bastard, I'll fucken kill ya."

The next blow caught him on the shoulder, which hurt like hell but gave him enough time to scramble to his feet before she launched herself at him again. She slipped in the blood and near-ly tripped over the prostrate figure on the floor. It was enough to give Jack the edge he needed. He couldn't bring himself to punch a woman, but this was a special case, so he grabbed her by the hair which had come loose from her bun and swung her around, driving her headfirst into the crockery cabinet, smash-ing the thin ply doors and scattering cheap china all over the bench and floor. That slowed her down, and he got another hand onto her dress and drove her into the cabinet again, then swung her round, put a full face hold on her, and thumped her head into the timber wall as hard as he could. It took four goes before she dropped the husband-tamer and went limp, slumping to the floor amid the smashed plates and corn flakes.

Jack leant back on the sink taking in the mess. "Bloody hell, what a fucken family!" he muttered, as he wiped his nose and straightened his tie.

Enough was enough. He reefed Terry up from the floor, sat

him in the only unbroken chair in the room, then pulled out his gun, spun the cylinders and pointed it at his head.

"Right, you fucken weasel. Let's have the story."

He was, of course, the deserter son. He'd taken the offer from the recruiting sergeant at the courthouse to stay out of jail, then leapt off the train taking him north in the middle of the night when it stopped up near Innisfail. He got work he didn't like at all on a sugar farm, and met Aina – Mrs C – who was staying with relatives up there. She didn't know he was on the run at the time, and he didn't know she was married. It was a short-lived affair: being a bludger at heart, he'd gone back to hide out at mum's, and things had been nice and quiet until Aina turned up after another split with the hubby. It started to go bad very quickly: his mum hated all foreigners and made her life hell, and he got on the piss and smacked her around because she could go out and he couldn't, and he figured a few bruises might keep her inside more. Why did she hang around and put up with it? Jack wanted to know.

"She had nowhere else to go, and she needed protecting," Terry mumbled. "Her husband wanted to kill her."

"Hold up!" said Jack. "The husband wanted to kill her?"

"Yeah," said Terry. "She did something, I dunno what, and he swore he'd kill her. That's why she's here."

"But he's dead!"

"Since when?"

"Over a week now," said Jack. "She doesn't know?"

"Well, I'd have no hold on her anymore if she did," said Terry, which was honest enough of him.

Jack twirled the revolver in his fingers. "Alright, young feller me lad, here's the go. You head back to your unit and join your cobbers defending your country, or one of two things will happen: I'll dob ya in to the redcaps and you'll go into a military prison, which believe me you don't want to do – or I'll shoot ya meself. How's that sound?"

"Not much chop!" blubbered the youth, all bravado gone, as his mother groaned and tried to rouse herself, but only slid further down the wall.

"Mate, you've got an hour to get into Vic Barracks and hand yourself in. You can walk it easy. They'll be tough, but that's not as bad as it could be. It's better to give yourself up, believe me."

"But I might get killed."

"You might not, too. But you definitely will if you cross me. I don't care. I've done it before. And you know what? I fucken like it! So don't tempt me. Put your boots back on and go and be a man. You don't have to be like your father. Here's a chance to be worthwhile . . . I'd advise ya to take it."

As the youth dolefully packed his bag, sobbing quietly, Jack rubbed the lump on his head and pondered the problem of dear old mum. She was definitely a handful, and harder to reason with than a taipan. As soon as Terry was out the door, he grabbed some sash cord from the window that had been shattered in the struggle and tied her up, gagged her with a greasy dishcloth, then dragged her into the bathroom and lumped her into the bath. Once he was outside, he went straight to the phone booth on the corner and dialled Len.

"I want that fucken car now!" he barked.

Something in his tone worked. He picked up a much better one, a fairly recent Ford, half an hour later and drove round to Vic Barracks. The Provost Marshall's office wouldn't say whether a T. Cox had handed himself in or not, but the deskie gave him a wink and said they weren't looking for him at this stage. Maybe there was a spark of goodness in the kid. Or maybe he'd light out again. The main thing was that he was gone, and the dog could see the rabbit. Next stop was the church.

15

He didn't muck around this time, just went straight in and sat down next to her. She moved away a couple of feet in shock.

"Don't worry," he said quietly. "I'm here to help."

"I don't know you."

"Well I know who you are, Mrs Callaghan. Or may I call you Aina?

"What do you want?"

"I need to talk to you about your husband."

"Why?"

A movement at the back of the church caught his eye and as he stood up he could see the shadowy form of Delaney shoot off like a cockroach does when the lights come on.

"Can we get out of here? I have a car."

"Here is safe."

"I wouldn't count on that, to tell you the truth."

"Why should I go with you?"

"Look, I really want to help you."

"Why is this? You don't know me!"

"I know a bit about you, and it's important we continue this somewhere else."

She stood up, accepting his hand on her arm, and followed

him outside. He ushered her into the back seat, where it was a bit more spacious and, since he'd had the heater running, nice and warm.

Honesty was the best policy. "I'm a detective hired to investigate your husband."

"You find me for him!" she gasped, looking around for a way out.

He held his hands up, palms outward.

"No no, not at all. Don't be frightened. He can't hurt you now."

She looked at him wide-eyed. "What does this mean?"

It had to be said. "He's dead."

She sank back in the seat, still looking wildly around, as if not believing it. "How did this happen?"

"Well, at this stage it looks like he killed himself."

"*Suicidio, no!* Is impossible!"

"How come?"

"He was a strong man, a bad man . . . but strong in the heart. He would never do this!"

"Well, he was found hanging in his flat.'

"When?"

"About ten days ago now."

She started sobbing and leant against him. He gently put his arm around her and patted her shoulder in comfort, but it was dangerously close to an embrace, and his blood started pumping a bit quicker. Shit, he thought, better pull the horse up or a man's gunna look bad real quick. He tried to keep his mind on the more gruesome aspects of things to keep the swelling night tackle under control.

"I have to tell you something."

"What?" she sniffled.

"The priest here . . . he knows."

"Padre Delaney?" she sat up again, "No!"

"Yes indeed. Why do you think he said nothing to you?"

"This is impossible!"

"Why would I lie? We can go and ask him if you like . . . but look, let's go back a bit. What are you doing in this church every day? I thought you were an anarchist."

Her eyes widened. "You really are the detective, señor. What don't you know?"

"Quite a lot. Now, the priest . . . this church . . . what's the story?"

"It was the *pesadillas!* How you say? The nightmares!"

Apparently Bill Callaghan had not been able to banish the memories of the massacre, and whatever else he'd got up to in Spain. He would thrash around at night, and the story gradually came out. She didn't know he'd been at Tarém; she was horrified to learn that the man she shared her bed with had been in charge.

"It was terrible the things that were done . . . to cut off the priest's head, and make the young boys put their tongues on his *pene*, his organ! And then to cut their throats . . . this was too much of a thing for me. It is beyond a sin. I came to the church to confess my *contaminación* by this man. I lie with him, but the marriage is not of the church, and he has done these things! What will happen to my soul? Padre Delaney helped so much with my absolution, but the penance *I* must do. It will never leave me."

Jack leaned back against the car door. Shit, it was getting darker all the time, this yarn. Old Bill had really gone to town over there, but the circularity of it all defied belief. Here's the wife confessing the sins of the husband to the priest who probably caused it all in the first place. What a fucken small world.

"Can you clear up something? I thought you hated the Church."

"Si, the church in Spain is very bad and holds down the people. But this is not the fault of our Lord. This is the faith of my parents, even if some who believe it are bad. I could not live without it. What will happen to my soul when I die? I cannot escape these feelings, so I come back to the church in this country. They are different here, closer to the word of the Saviour."

"You think so, eh?"

He sat back slightly rubbing his chin. "So you just chanced on this church, and the good Father here never told you he knew Bill from years ago?"

"No. He went around to my husband to try and save his soul. He said this was such a sin he had to go beyond the rules . . . But he never say that he know Bill from before."

"So neither of 'em mentioned the fact they went back the best part of twenty years?"

"No. Bill, he just beat me, and this is why I run to my cousins in the north . . ."

" . . . where you hooked up with Terry the gutless wonder."

"How do you know *him*?"

"Insurance, remember?"

A puzzled look flitted across her face. "This was you?"

"Yep, I'm your guardian angel, love, but we'll get to that in a minute. Go on."

"Yes, Terry was nice for a short time, until I find out he is a coward and I run away from him too. But when I come back to my husband, he is still crazy and threatens to kill me. What can I do? I am disgraced with my people for being with the Communists, my cousins call me a *puta* for going with Terry and say they should kill me for this shame . . . Where can I go except back to Terry and his mother."

She broke down again and he cuddled her genuinely.

"Yeah, well I've sorted those bastards out, so don't worry

about them."

She looked up at him through the dark curls that framed her bruised yet beautiful face. "How do you mean?"

"I mean I went round and gave young Terry a lesson in how to behave, and had a word with his mother while I was at it."

She shuddered at the mention. "This woman is a beast! She hits me, too."

"Yeah, well that won't happen any more. You don't ever have to set foot there again. I'll sort out a place you can stay, then we'll get your things from that shithole, and you're out of there forever, alright?"

She held him tighter, sobbing quietly. He was a goner by that stage. He'd bottled up most emotions over the years, and when the floodgates opened he wasn't sure how to handle it.

They sat there quietly as a light rain pattered against the windscreen.

16

One thing about Vi: she was a good sport. She didn't bat an eyelid when Jack walked in out of the rain with the exotic beauty and put the bite on her for the spare room at the front that was being held for the business type from down south. He only showed up once a month anyway. She got the tea on, ran a hot bath, and sorted out some clean clothes her daughter had left behind when she went to Sydney with the WACs. Once Aina was in the bathroom soaking away the tears, he grabbed his coat off the rack.

"I'll be back directly," said Jack, "I gotta go and clean up some mess. Can you tuck her in for me?"

Vi looked at him darkly. "Not like you to put a sheila that far from ya midnight grasp. What's the story? Gone all honourable for a change?"

"She's had a hard time . . . I got *some* principles, ya know."

"Not that I've ever seen where there's panties concerned."

"Yeah, well this is different."

"Building Rome, are we?" Vi guffawed.

"I just fucken might be, yeah."

It only took ten minutes in the car and he was back at Sloth House. He kicked in the door of the front flat, and quickly found the boxes of cheap gin and brandy. There was a whole room full: Old Ma Cox would have been pulling down a tidy quid with this lot. He opened a bottle and took a swig: it was awful. He strolled down the verandah with it and pushed the end door open. It was still ajar, just as he'd left it, so none of her tenants had seen fit to investigate the shenanigans of a few hours earlier. Bashing and crashing accompanied by foul language was probably the nightly show round these parts. Mrs Cox was still in the bath; she'd not been able to extricate herself from her bonds despite some obvious struggling. The eyes that glowered at him were fierce. He reached for the rag in her mouth.

"Now I'm gunna take this out, but if you start yelling I'll shove it back in and come back tomorrah, fair enough?"

She nodded. He removed the gag. She licked her lips.

"You fucken arsehole. I'll kill ya."

"No ya won't. I'm the one with the gun. Want a drink?"

She nodded again. He shoved the neck of the gin bottle roughly into her mouth, and she gulped it angrily.

"Thanks for nothing, shitbox."

"You're nice. I could go for a girl like you."

"I wouldn't let you up me for a million quid!"

"I'd need twice that to even think about it. Anyway, let's cut the blarney, shall we? What happens if I let you loose."

"Whattya reckon? Where's my boy?"

"Back in the army doing what he's supposed to, so rubbish like you can walk around free."

"You cunt."

"Woah, that's lovely. You're a fucken classic, you are."

"No one asked ya to come round here and stick ya nose in. You'll pay, brother."

"This is getting difficult. You're too fucken heavy to take

down the river and drown like the fucken rat that y'are!" He got the gun out. "I might just have to plug ya and be done with it."

"You wouldn't be game."

"No? I'm a fast talker. I'd come up with some excuse, and really, who'd miss ya?"

He wrapped the revolver in a filthy towel from the floor, then pointed it at her temple and pulled the trigger. The sharp click made her flinch so hard she belted her head on the tap. He spun the cylinder and pulled it once more. A puddle of urine trickled down toward the plughole as it clicked again, so she hadn't twigged the thing wasn't loaded.

"Shit, you're lucky. I'd better up the odds." He ostentatiously filled the chambers with some rounds from his other pocket, leaned over, and put the barrel in the middle of her forehead: "Can't we just be friends? There's no need for all this. I mean, I can have the bulls here in ten minutes loading up all your grog, and you'll do time, I don't wanna do that if I don't have to."

"That won't happen. I'm looked after."

"Not by the blokes I know, so don't get too fucken cocky. You're a nobody and a fucken parasite. I can put you in a deep hole, don't worry, but I don't need any extra aggravation in me life at this point. So let's just stay out of each other's way, deal?"

She nodded, the fight seemingly gone out of her.

"I'm going to go and get her things now, so not one peep out of you till I'm finished, then I walk out of here and our paths never cross again."

A mumbled reply was all he got as he went and grabbed a suitcase and shoved anything remotely feminine he could find into it. As he left, he stopped at the entrance to the bathroom and threw a breadknife into the tub. "This'll get ya loose if ya use some imagination."

A couple of blinds were pulled back once he got outside, and wide-eyed faces followed him out to the car. But he didn't care who saw what now: his life had turned a corner.

When he got back to the boarding house, Vi was sitting up listening to the radio, and the door to the spare room was closed.

"She's asleep," Vi said.

"That's good," he replied.

Vi walked over till she was looking him right in the eye.

"What are you doin', Jack? I've never seen you like this. Ya haven't gone mushy on me, have ya? I mean, she's a good sort and she'll brush up real nice, by the look of her, but I dunno . . . Be careful, and this isn't the green-eyed monster talking."

He put his hand on her shoulder. "We go back a fair way, Vi, and I won't bullshit ya. Me eyes are wide open, but I think I'm a sucker for this one."

She put her hand on her hip as she stood back and looked him up and down. "You do what you want."

"Thanks, love. Don't worry, at least I know I'm never too old to be made a fool of by a woman. But who knows? We could all be dead tomorrow."

She went and stood by the sink, and looked out the window. The conversation was over.

Once he was back in his room, Jack pulled out a bottle of rum and a pad and pencil, and sat down on the bed. It was time to do some thinking. There was a thread running through all of this, but he still couldn't find it.

So many imponderables. Too many coincidences. Jack never kept notes; it was a bad habit, but at least he had a reasonable memory. He started drawing little circles and timelines connecting them up; it didn't take long before one thing seemed to be growing more and more pivotal. He picked up the phone; Simpson was in his office.

"Me again."

"What? Got something new for me already?"

"No, something old . . . Can you find out where our mate O'Reilly was stationed in the late war years?"

"Back when he walked the beat? That's not too hard, but I need a good reason why."

"Murder."

"Oh no. Not your bloody commo who went the drop again, is it?"

"Yep. O'Reilly took the call."

"What?"

"Yep. I was keeping it up me sleeve . . . The old dear next door told me. He was there, first on the spot. What are the odds on that, seeing as he's in Armed Hold-up and not Homicide? Why would they be called in at all?"

"You're drawing a long bow here, mate."

"I know that, but humour me, will ya? And while you're at it, where would the rope be?"

"What, the noose?"

"Yep."

"With whoever did the report."

"Who might that be? Or is that a silly question?"

"You do the sums, mate."

"Can you get hold of it?"

"Depends."

"On what."

"Lots of things, such as the bullshit I'm going to have to think up to go anywhere with this."

"Look, I can't remember who owes who what between us, so I'm not gunna start bleating, but here's a go: I got a fiver says that gangly fucken mongrel cut his straps out at Toowoomba. Whattya reckon?"

"Make it ten."

"Jeez, you're a hard man."

"No, I'm just confident this is a wild goose chase."

"Well if it is, you'll have a bit of spare folding. Spend it wisely on that divorcee you been squirin' about the district and ya might get her legs in the air."

"Struth, you're fucken low! don't you think about anything else? Gimme a coupla days."

"Mate, you're a champion!"

"Hey, you're the one with a head like a spark plug, so pull it in. See ya later."

Jack hung up and kept drawing circles and lines, and then it hit him . . . Tarém. How did old Callaghan know his boy was involved if he hadn't spoken to him for bloody years? He picked up the phone again and got Len at home.

"Mate, remember those jokers who got ya the mail on Callaghan senior's building mob?"

"Yeah.'

"Mate, see if you can get them to dig up a bit of info on his early days. Say, twenty years back . . . Where did he start off and so forth."

"Why?"

"I'm tryin' not to weave too big a web here, but believe me it's all relevant. This is getting weirder by the day."

"This isn't some ploy to string out the job, is it?"

"Mate, money's got nothin' to do with it now. I smell a rat and I'm after the bastard."

"Fair enough, sport. I'll do what I can."

17

There's something special about the taste of fairy floss mixed with lipstick, and he got a nice gobful up on top of the ferris wheel. It was a promising development, and about time. Sideshow Alley had soaked up quite a few quid. The Ekka was going strong that year. They'd temporarily moved out a lot of the troops who'd been using the showgrounds as a staging area, and the bushies had come down in droves. A bit of bright lights and excitement does wonders during dark days, and all sorts were letting off steam.

He hadn't heard from either of his sources for a few days, and had used the break wisely. The phone was off the hook in the office, and with a nice stack of commo coin in his kick, he'd been hard at work on the widow.

They did the afternoon tea routine at Lennon's Hotel, with all the Yankee big brass and local nobs swanning about; rode the ferry out to Lone Pine, where she cuddled a koala; took in the sights from Mt Coot-tha; and generally did the courting couple routine. But every night it was back to the front room for her and the ceiling stare for him. It was a hard slog for Jack: he'd always been a fast worker, but he knew deep down he had to play this right; there was more than a quickie at stake. He kept it up for the best part of a week, with the full flush trip to the Show the crowning glory. Finally the long walk through Victoria Park, after they'd done with the laughing clowns, did the trick: he kissed her again under a tree in the dappled moonlight, and she went limp but pliant in his arms. It was on.

She didn't even look at the door of her own room as they went down the passageway, and she was breathing fast as she leant against the doorjamb while he fumbled with the key. The door was open in a flash and they tumbled onto the bed. There was no mucking around; she reached down and tore her panties aside and he drove straight into her through the remnants of the gusset, biting at the cleavage of the dress as they thrust roughly together. Then she flipped him over and started riding him in a frenzy. The dark tresses fell over her sweating face as she picked up the tempo, and Jack was doing his best to keep up without letting fly too early . . . but it couldn't last. As he watched in amazement, she tore her dress down off her shoulders, freeing her enormous breasts, which she grasped with both hands, pulling them upwards and together. She began feverishly licking her own nipples as she ground down on his pubic bone, and that was it. Jack went off like a skyrocket, and she let out a howl they would have heard in Queen Street, then collapsed over him, kissing his neck and face while her clamping muscles rhythmically milked out the last drops. Holy hell, he thought, as he realised he still had his coat on. I've got meself a handful here.

Jack was a drained man by morning, and was cheerfully hoeing into his breakfast when the sleeping arrangements came up for discussion. Vi was adamant that a bit of nookie here and there was one thing, but the two of them openly living in sin was beyond the pale for her establishment, even if Aina was a widow.

Jack could see her point, but his dick was doing the thinking. It was finally agreed that in the short term Aina would stay in the front room, to keep appearances up, and had to be back in there by dawn. But they'd have to find new premises as soon as poss, or do the decent thing. It was a temporary compromise, enough to keep the hounds on the leash and the door open for the big fella for now.

He left the women to do whatever they did during the day and headed in to the office He'd barely sat down when the phone rang. It was Jim Simpson, in very terse mode.

"Right. Ya got ya ten."

"Knew it!"

"Stop crowin', ya bastard. And by the way, the rope doesn't tell us much."

"Yeah? Have yez had a chandler give it a squiz?"

"Oh that's right, you're a detective, aren't ya? Well why don't you do just that? There's a package being dropped off this morning, there might be a surprise in it."

"You starting to believe me?"

"No, but who knows what evil lurks in the heart of men?"

"Fuck me, that's poetic."

"Not really. 'The Shadow knows . . .' "

"Who?"

"You know, the radio show. Me squeeze never misses it, likes a cup of tea and a sit down while it's on."

"That's nice – and a cheap night out. That should mean ya can pay ya gambling debts?"

"Don't get smart, you'll get ya money. Just keep me up to speed, alright?"

The sergeant who dropped off the package about an hour later never said a word, just glared at him like he was a turd in a punchbowl. Jack didn't know if it was from something in the past, or just on principle. No wonder no one liked coppers, he thought. How did I ever end up one?

There were ship's chandlers and shops full of nautical thinguma-bobs down around New Farm, so Jack drove down and parked near the Bulimba ferry, and strolled into one that backed on to the river. There was a stiff breeze coming off the water, and he was glad to get into the warmth and clutter.

Rope comes in many forms. A bewildering variety of cord-age hung about the shop as the young bloke behind the counter checked out the specimen Jack had brought.

"Well it's three-strand . . . What else do you want to know?"

"Is it definitely off a boat?"

"Might be, might not. There's no rogue's yarn."

"No what? Yarns? Ya gunna tell me a story?"

The young bloke let it go through to the keeper. "Rogue's yarn, it's a bit of black twine in the rope to tell ya the grading."

"Don't get too technical, mate. Just tell me where I'd get some like this from if I needed more."

Just then a much older man came in from the back.

"What are you on about, young Bill?" he barked. "That's only in manila two inches and over." He grabbed the specimen. "You've got a long way to go, son," he chuckled as he inspected it minutely. Jack had taken the liberty of undoing the noose so as not to colour the imagination, but the old fellow didn't seem the type to be fazed anyway.

"This has gotta be hemp for a start, and what's this?" he stopped and looked closely at the cut and frayed ends, first one, then the other.

"Aha!" he shouted, eyes gleaming. "This is a bell rope, mat-ey!"

"What, like in the cathedrals?"

"Yep. The old hunchback coulda swung on this one."

"How can ya tell?"

"The practiced eye, mate. See this bit of coloured wool here woven into the end? I'll bet me balls that's where the sally got cut off."

"Who's she when she's at home?"

"Mate – old joke, alright? The big woven handle's called a sally, and it's usually got red and blue wool through it. This is top quality, pre-stretched, three-strand flax hemp, and I reckon it's been cut off an old bell rope, never been near the sea. If ya wanna find where it came from, I'd be cockin' an ear for the sound of the bells."

"I owe yez a beer," Jack said as he rolled up the length and put it back in the shoebox.

"So who hung himself?" said the old bloke.

Jack turned in astonishment.

"How in fuck's name . . . ?"

"I've tied a few knots over the last fifty-odd years, digga," was the reply. "I can see where a slipknot's been. That was round some bloke's neck or I'm a Chinaman. Happy hunting!"

Jack pushed his hat back off his forehead and looked askance at the old-timer.

"Worse things happen at sea."

"See ya round for that beer," the old man smiled, and went back into the dusty confines of the shop. The young bloke stood there looking silly as Jack walked out and back to the car. A tram heading back into the city clanged a warning as he crossed the road, and he laughed at the sound while shaking his head.

Bells . . . church . . . He shoulda known.

18

He didn't bother with the holy water at the entrance, just strode right through to the sacristy. There was no one around, and he kept opening doors until he found himself at the bottom of the small bell tower. It was pretty dusty, and stacks of candle boxes lined the walls along with other bits of worshipful paraphernalia.

Under a bit of hessian was a pile of rope, looking pretty frayed in places, and jammed down the back was a heavier piece, about a yard long, with coloured wool in it, The clean cut on one end matched the rope Jack had perfectly, He stood up, grinning: Got the bastard. How fucken slack can ya be? Evidence lying round just waiting to picked up . . . what a dill!

A noise behind him made him whirl around. It was his old mate Delaney.

"So you're a burglar as well," intoned the priest.

"That's a bit rich comin from a murderin' kiddie fiddler. Anyway, the door was open."

"As it is to all God's children."

"Look, fucken spare me that guff, alright? You're a goner, mate."

"Really? What do you think you've found.'

"A direct link between you and the murder."

"He killed himself."

"Bullshit."

"What is so hard to believe? He was a troubled soul."

"You were there."

"You're right. I was – after he was dead."

"Stop fucken lying! This puts you there beforehand."

"No it doesn't."

Jack was getting exasperated. "Look, I've got ya cold."

"You've got nothing. That rope was old and had to be re-placed. William must have taken it."

"Get out!"

"Prove otherwise."

"I can do just that."

"How?"

"The oil on the body."

Delaney suddenly looked worried. "Oil?"

"Yeah, the oil of extreme unction was on the body, mate. They found it."

"So?"

"Well, you can't give a suicide that sacrament, can ya?"

Delaney was silent.

"So you either broke your own law, or you killed him and hung him up to make it look like suicide. You'll fucken go, mate."

Delaney sat down on a rough stool next to the wall. "Look he really did kill himself, you know. He was a very troubled man."

"Do you wonder why?"

"He did some terrible things."

"And you haven't?"

"I have truly repented for my sins."

"That's handy for you. Less so for those young fellers over in Spain who copped it in the neck because you couldn't keep ya tool to yourself. Ever thought about that?"

"That's the will of the Lord. I'm not to blame for that terrible sin."

"Aw, get fucked. I can't believe this! Tell me what happened or I'll fucken string you up right now, so ya know how it feels."

"You won't do that, but I'll tell you anyway. I'm the one with the burden here. I did give him extreme unction, but while he was still alive."

"How come?"

"It's supposed to be given before the soul has actually departed, you know."

"So you didn't cut him down . . . You left him hangin'?"

"No, *before* he did it, so his soul would be at rest."

"What? Then you watched him top himself?"

"That's right. But you can't prove it."

"So you told him it was alright to go ahead after you'd given your blessing?"

"So to speak."

The priest sat back deflated, as if a huge load had been lifted with the telling, but that didn't impress Jack too much.

"You're a fucken cold one, mate. You fuck this bloke's life up right from the start, and then calmly convince him to top himself when it all comes unstuck in the end!"

"He needed the release. It was merciful."

"I can't believe I'm hearing this! You sat and watched him do it?"

"He needed to pay for his sins. I could not stand in the way of the Lord's judgement."

Jack leaned against the wall. "Mate, I've been around a bit, and seen some grim capers, but this is something else, I gotta tell ya. Don't you feel anything any remorse or guilt?"

"None at all."

"You're fucken insane. What about your own laws or whatever – isn't it a mortal sin?"

A strange light seemed to shine from the man's eyes; he stared at Jack like something in an aquarium. "I am prepared to be judged."

I've had enough, Jack thought. "You will be. I'll take this to the cops," he said as he left the room. "Assisting a suicide is still a crime."

"Do what you like. I'll answer to the Lord and my own conscience in that order. As for the rest, I don't care."

Jack didn't look back as went down the steps of the church, but he knew he wouldn't go back into it or any other church again, and neither would Aina if they were going to keep on with it.

19

It was well after five when Jack pulled up at the Hamilton mansion. The tree-lined street seemed darker than the early gathering gloom allowed, so his headlights lit up the front entrance, alerting those inside to his approach.

The butler had the door open before he reached it. "I'm sorry, sir. You're not welcome here."

"I'll go right through you, pal. Is that what you want?"

Callaghan appeared. "Let him in."

They went down the hall into a room where a couple of men in robes sat in large leather chairs. The room was dark, and so were the expressions of everyone in it.

"You won't drop it will you, Munro?" came a voice from behind him. O'Reilly sauntered in from outside and leant on the doorjamb, smoking a pipe.

"Well wacko!" said Jack. "The gang's all here! Let's have a corroboree!"

"What do you want?" Callaghan asked calmly as he sat down, leaving Jack standing alone in the centre of the room.

"I know the whole story now. And a fucken sad and horrible one it is too. You lot are a disgrace."

"How so?" said one of the cassocked figures.

"Let's go back twenty years or so," Jack started. "The good Father Delaney is happily dipping his wick into the altar boys out Toowoomba way, one of whom, young Billy Callaghan, gets a sore arse and tells Mum. His old man here goes up to the school – breathing fire, no doubt – but not before calling the local copper, one O'Reilly, who's propping up the wall over there as I speak.

"Now this sort of thing is bad for business. Young fellers getting beaten round the date tends to upset most people, but by crikey, we can't have all this bad publicity now, can we? So I reckon some candle carrier further up the chain of command sorts out a solution. Delaney gets sent to some out of the way spot for being a naughty boy; as for Mr Callaghan, well he's pretty handy with a hammer and nails, and we need a new church hall down the road here, so how about you start up your own firm, Michael, and knock a few buildings together for us? It'll be sweet. No more to be said. Lots of backslapping and ha-de-fucken-ha.

"And young Bill, what about him? Well, life's full of hurdles. He'll be right. He'll get over it.

"Well he fucken didn't, did he? He never forgot, and when he got older he turned and went as far as he could from everything you lot stand for. And who can blame him? The only thing is: he kept on going, and one day in Spain he went right over the top, and a lot of innocent young fellers just like he'd been once, before *you* lot got hold of him, died pretty horrible fucken deaths, from what I can gather.

"But is that the end of it? Not by a long shot. Years later, our mate Father Delaney is having a quiet gasper in the church one arvo, where he's been slotted away from the general gaze – but, you might note, not too far from the prospect of young meat in his other job as footy coach. Anyway, who should walk in but this distressed woman whose husband is havin' nightmares about some horror show back in the war over in Spain. And whattya know, isn't coincidence a funny thing, it's our Bill, back from perdition, and a very troubled soul to boot. Delaney, brazen as you please, goes over to his place and starts stirring up this poor bastard about the state of his soul, and what he's done – and drives the bugger to the point of killing himself. Now, he won't have gone off on his tod and done this. Oh, no. He's reported in to our gang here, and you lot have all gone, *Dear oh fucken dear, that's all very dreadful, but this bloke has to pay for his sins*. So Delaney goes back over there with the rope and all, and convinces the poor mad bastard that if he gives him this last rites shit or whatever it is, he can then go and hang himself and his soul be will be sweet in the afterlife. I wouldn't be surprised if the old cunt hung on to his feet to make sure the knot was tight enough.

"And you," he pointed at Callaghan, "you did this to your own flesh and blood! You're all fucken disgusting. This is the rankest caper I've ever fucken heard of."

O'Reilly tapped his pipe against his heel outside the door, came inside, and stood straight in front of Jack. "Interesting yarn, Munro. Pity you can't back any of it up."

"That I can," he replied. "I've got evidence."

"Who'll you give it to?"

"The police."

"Believe me, all they have to do is ask where you got it from, and any decent barrister will shoot it down in flames. Simpson should have known better."

"At least he did something," replied Jack."Alright, I'll go to the church big boys."

"Oh, I don't think that'll be necessary," O'Reilly said. "The Archbishop here's heard your fairy story."

The small man in the corner, lips pursed, folded his hands as if praying, then rested his chin on his two index fingers as he ruminated before speaking. "Even if all this were true, which I doubt, one more dead Communist can't be a great loss. And sometimes one has to break the law to serve it. Wouldn't you, especially, agree?"

Jack looked at them all and shook his head.

"I've never been a religious man, and you know what? I thank fuck for that. I don't know why we bother fighting wars. You're all the fucken same in the end. It's all about money and power, and fuck the little bloke. Literally, you make me fucken spew."

He walked out, seething with helpless rage, but turned as he reached the door. "You think you won? But I'll tell me fucken story."

"Talk's cheap," said O'Reilly, pointing the pipe at him. "No one's gunna listen."

20

There was a back room at the Imperial, and Duesie was waiting in it when Jack marched in.

They called him Duesie because his last name was Duesenberg, like the luxury American car, but he was actually descended from some German settlers who'd come to the Lockyer Valley in the 1800s. He'd never ridden in one, but had been around plenty of places where they did in his role as society columnist for the *Courier*. It was a cushy number compared to his years on the police beat, and he'd got the gig as a sort of retirement package-cum-payoff as he slowly recovered from a near-fatal stabbing he received covering a domestic out at Pinkenba. They'd met at a few car prangs and dead 'uns when Jack was still wearing the size tens, and, as is the way of such things, soon got into the habit of polishing off a fair amount of sauce when nothing much else was happening.

They weren't close mates any more, for various reasons now forgotten, but still on good terms, which didn't go unnoticed by the newspaperman. His family had been around long enough to have lost most vestiges of their original German culture, so no real suspicion fell upon them once Hitler got rolling . . . still, there was still a fair bit of subtle standoffishness about, but that was one thing you never got from Munro.

Duesie listened intently while Jack told the story again, and sat back pensively when he'd finished. "You don't seriously think that'll get to print, do ya?" he asked.

"Well I was sort of hopin'."

"Mate, don't even dream about it. They wouldn't touch it."

"You don't know."

"I fucken do know."

"Will ya have a go?"

"Mate, I gotta nice life."

"Yeah, all them parties and shit . . . but don't ya miss the real stuff?"

"The real stuff cost me a lung, sport, and half me nerves as well."

"Yeah, but not ya fucken balls, as I recall. Or did it?"

Duesie rubbed his chin and pushed his hat back. He never took it off, even indoors.

"I'll write it up and give it to the news editor for ya. That's all I can do, alright? That way at least it's out and about. People will talk, even if it doesn't go to print, if that means anything."

"Not much. Can I have a copy?"

"Sure you can, but why? Don't ya trust me?"

"Not that. It just means that I don't have to be peckin' away at a typewriter, makin' up a report for them that's hired me. I don't wanna tell it again, really. It shits me too much. You can have all me notes. I don't wanna know about this anymore, to be honest."

Duesie drained his beer, put the various bits into his briefcase, and held out a slightly trembling hand. They shook, and Jack noticed his grip wasn't what it used to be. It was pretty limp, in fact, and if he didn't already know him well, Jack woulda been put right off by it. He sat down again after Duesie left and swallowed the last of his beer while ruminating on what makes some blokes able to take just about anything, and others not.

Jack was about to order another one when he noticed it was nearly seven. There was a warm woman waiting at home, he reminded himself. She might drain a bit of the poison out of him.

The welcome was vigorous, and afterwards they snuggled up under the covers, luxuriating in one another's warmth: rooting was more fun in cold weather, a bit more cuddly, instead of all that lathering up like a racehorse on a summer's night; he hated that.

It was lucky he was closest to the door. He saw the barrel as it came through before the figure holding it appeared, and he threw himself across Aina as the first blast hit him in the back with a searing pain. They both rolled off the bed, tangled in the bloody sheets, as the tall figure loomed over them and fired again as he blacked out.

21

The echo of footsteps brought him out of the never-never land he'd been in, and he realised he was looking at a polished floor. It hurt when he tried to move. As he came to, it soon dawned on him he was lying face down, and that hard smell of cotton sheets was right under his cheek.

He looked around and the wardsman noticed him. A nurse arrived soon after, and told him to lie still as she gave him a drink through a straw. It had a strange, lemony taste and he asked dazedly what it was.

"We call it conch," said the nurse. "I can't stand it, but then I s'pose anything wet would taste good after a dry spell like you've had."

"How long have I been here?"

"This is the second day," said the nurse. "Doctor will fill you in very soon. He's been notified you're awake."

A white coat swished up on cue. "Ah, Mr Munro," he said, chart in hand. "Back from the brink, I see."

"What brink, mate?"

"Yes, well . . . Don't recall much, I see. You were shot, you know."

"Well I know how that feels. It isn't the first time."

"Mmm, returned man, aren't you? Saw a few scars. Just as well, I'd say. You lost a fair bit of blood there, even though the vitals were in no real danger."

"Aina?"

"Yes, look . . . She's in the women's ward. I'm afraid I can't tell you more than that, as it is a police matter."

"Yeah right, of course. But what happened, who . . .?"

"Can't say, I'm afraid, but I'll ring the chap looking after your case, or whatever they call it. He'll pop down and fill you in."

"Look, I want to see her."

"Out of the question right now, old boy. But she's in no danger, so don't worry."

"What's the damage?"

"Oh, of course, how remiss of me. You sustained a large flesh wound on the upper back, all the shot . . ."

"What! Not a bullet?"

"No, shot. Took bloody ages to dig it out. A right mess, You were like a seriously buggered game bird, to be frank, but there you go . . . It sort of glanced off the scapula."

"How's that?"

"The shoulder blade. It peeled off a rather large chunk, which we've sewn back on with only limited damage to the musculature. All in all, you're a lucky chap. A slightly different angle and it could have got you in the neck and the carotid artery, in which case we wouldn't be talking. Or a bit the other way and you'd be a cripple. So all up not a bad result, considering the initial blood loss. The shock from that might well have done another bloke in."

"I was fucken shocked alright."

"It's a medical term, and it kills more people than you'd think. But looking forward, you'll be stiff and sore for quite a while and need a bit of physio for the arm . . . I assume you're right-handed."

"Yep."

"That's a pity, but you should come good in time . . . Anyway, I'll pop in later and see how you are, but I'd say you'll be out of here within the week."

The doctor swirled around and took off down the aisle between the beds, while Jack lay there fretting. Who in hell . . . ? And Aina, what about her? Fuck, what a mess. Who was it . . . and why? Them fucken priests . . . He cursed and tried to get up, but a nurse came and jabbed him in the buttock. A warm glow swept through him and he relaxed again. He'd know soon enough, and the bastards would pay.

He came around a bit later, and spied Jim Simpson and Ted Duesenberg deep in conversation out on the verandah, the sibilant whispers of the poinsettias in the breeze masking their conversation.

Jack decided to interrupt their cosy natter: "What are you bastards up to? Come to pick me corpse?"

"Shit," said Simpson. "It's back."

They pulled up chairs next to the bed and sat down where he could see them.

"Believe me now?" said Jack. "I told ya the whole thing stunk, now look what happened."

"What are you on about?"

"The priests and O'Reilly . . . They nearly done me in!"

"You're delirious."

"I am fucken not, those bastards . . ."

"Didn't you see who shot ya? It wasn't them, ya fucken mug, so settle down!"

"I saw nothin', mate. It was in the back, you might observe! So . . . who?"

"A Mrs Cox."

Jack's jaw could have caught flies.

"You're fucken kiddin'!"

"Nope. She strolled in and let yez both have it."

"I don't believe it!"

"Believe it, pal. And you're both bloody lucky she only had a
.410, or else you'd have been goners, I reckon."

"So Aina's alright?"

"Ah well, you better talk to the doctors about that. You only
copped a flesh wound, sizable though it is, but old Val gave it to
the girl point blank, from what I can gather. But as I say, she's
still with us."

Jack tried to roll over and sit up. "I gotta see her."

"In good time, mate. So what was your connection with her."

"Who, me girl?"

"Val Cox."

"Fucken ask *her*."

"We can't."

"How come?"

"Well your landlady's a dab hand with a griddle, it seems.
She came in when she heard the commotion and clocked Val
over the noggin just as she was about to put a load into yours.
The only thing is, she put a bit too much into the swing and
managed to drive a shard of skullbone clean into the brainstem
of Ol' Ma Cox, and now she's a fucken cabbage. So you owe Vi
a big one, old mate."

"Shit. I didn't think I'd pissed her off that much. She hated
Aina, why would she care if she was with *me?*"

"Ah," said Simpson, "I shoulda known ya dong was involved."

Duesie butted in.

"Mate, I made a few inquiries where this lout couldn't, and it appears that the son copped it in New Guinea."

"Oh right. Well that's a turn-up . . . at least he did something worthwhile."

"Well you'd hope so, but not really. He did a runner first time he came under fire, it seems. Except the silly cunt didn't know what was where, and bolted straight into open ground where a Jap sniper had him for lunch. Mrs Cox got the telegram and flipped, and as Jim here says, the only piece she could snaffle was a bird gun, or else it coulda been a lot worse."

"So the priest had nothing to do with it?"

"Doesn't look that way," Jim said. "And while we're on the subject: when did you last see the good Father?"

"'Bout lunchtime that day. Why?"

"Well, he's gone to meet his maker."

"What! How?"

"Drowned."

"Break it down!"

"No, fair dink," said Duesie. "He went after a lost football at training last night and fell into Kedron Brook. There's a deep hole there near the playing fields, and he got tangled in some reeds, apparently . . . and there ya go."

"Mate, I can't take all of this in at once. Who saw this happen?"

"Well, no one . . . it's what they figured. He was packing up after all the lads had choofed off home, and when he didn't show up back at the priory someone went down to look for him. The shed was still open, and then a search was mounted."

"What, so sudden?"

"Yep, the coppers were called."

"Who by?"

"One of the club committee."

Jack could see Simmo looking agitated and shifting in his

seat.

"And who might that have been?"

Duesie coughed politely and mumbled, "Uh . . . Inspector O'Reilly."

Jack glared hard at Simpson.

"Don't look at *me*. Fuck ya!" he reponded.

Jack laughed. "What a fucken show! No one knows nothin', eh? And a bird can't sing underwater! Well, good riddance! They musta been a bit more worried than they let on. Anyway, bugger it. Who cares? When can I see me sheila? That's more important to me than all this shit."

The two men got up. "We'll go see her doc for ya," Jim said.

"Before ya go," he asked, "will Vi be charged?"

"Yeah, probably. But it's just a formality; most likely she won't go away for it."

"Just as fucken well," Jack muttered. "Go see what you can do for us."

They let him out of bed under protest an hour or so later and wheeled him in to see Aina. She looked crook: her hair lay limp on the pillow and she was deathly pale. She was still hooked up to some tubes. He thought. Shit, what a pair of crocks! But at least we're still here.

Her eyes opened, then widened when she saw him leaning forward in the wheelchair so he didn't touch the back of it.

"How are ya?"

"Do you love me, Jack?"

"Yeah, I s'pose."

"Can you say this?"

"What?"

"That you love me?"

"Do I have to? You know I do."

"Please say this."

"Why?"

"I need you to say it."

"Actions speak louder than words, don't they?"

"Not to a woman, Jack. Say it."

He looked around to see if anyone could hear, and then said real fast: "Yeah-I-love-ya-alright."

Aina smiled. "Is good enough."

"Good. What was that about?"

"This woman. Jack, when she shoot me . . ." She started crying. "Maybe I don't have any baby now."

"What? You can't have been pregnant already!"

"No, but for the future."

He put his head in his hands. "Look, don't worry about any of that now. You're alive, we're alive, that's all that matters."

A doctor came in as they sat holding hands. "Can I see you . . . Mr Munro, is it? Are you a relative?"

"No, but you can take it as read that her interests are paramount to me at the moment. Will that do ya? Now what's the rundown on her condition?"

"I see," said the doctor rather sniffily. "Well if we could just go outside for a minute."

Jack wheeled himself out into the corridor gingerly, marvelling at the doctor's complete lack of interest in his progress. "You can't give us a push, can ya, doc?" he asked sarcastically.

The doctor looked at him as if he'd been asked to eat shit with a toothpick . . . it was obviously an underling's job. Once they were out of earshot, the white coat resumed the conversation.

"Well, the injuries are mainly confined to the left side below just below the navel. Ummm . . ."

"Go on."

"It appears that there has been damage to the fallopian tubes and the ovary on that side."

"So what are you telling me?"

'Well, if the damage sustained by the uterus isn't too severe, she may still be able to conceive. But if there are complications, then I'm afraid that a hysterectomy may well be in order."

"So . . . no kids, eh?"

"It's unlikely, I'm afraid."

"Alright. Well, let's not raise the subject for now if we can avoid it. Concentrate on getting her up and about, eh?"

The doctor shut his folder and nodded, and Jack went back in to sit with her until they turfed him out.

22

They let him out three days later.

The constant trek over to his girl's bedside had been tough, but he was motivated. The third time he gave the chair the flick and walked, so by the end of his stay he was fairly mobile, if hardly fighting fit.

When he got home, his room had been cleaned up, but the mood was bit grim, what with Vi having been charged. After a day or two he rang Len and organised a meet, as much to get out of the house as anything. He needed to settle up as well. The comrades owed him a bit, and they'd taken the car back, so the taxi bills to and from the General twice a day at visiting hours were punishing his wallet. They had a few beers as Jack outlined the sorry saga, and Clancy O'Dea started ranting and raving about power and corruption.

Jack pointed out that perhaps Stalin's Russia wasn't the best example of an alternative to what was on offer in the wide brown land. "You can call Curtin a dill without being sent to a labour camp, brother!"

Len interjected to settle things down. "If you look at it one way, at least the priest got his comeuppance, even if it was at the hands of the state."

"Hold on," said Jack, " I'm not havin' that. It was bloody rogue elements of the *state*, as you call it."

Clancy wouldn't let go. "Well the structure allows for such deviation in order to suppress the masses."

"Righto," replied Jack. "This is a business meeting, not a political one."

"We're paying for your time here, and we'll decide what's discussed."

"Not any more, ya don't. Here's me bill."

His demeanour was forthright, and Len raised his eyebrows at Clancy, who pulled a money belt from around his waist and started peeling off tenners, saying he still felt that the story should be told, to let the public know how things really worked. Jack handed over a copy of Duesie's story, which of course hadn't hit the headlines. The death of Delaney had seen to that – rather conveniently, as Jack saw it – but what could you do.

"It's been written, but no bugger will print it."

After a bit more argy-bargy about that and the general principles involved, as opposed to the reality, he called stumps. All things considered, they went away satisfied: the suspicions that had led them to put him on the case had been confirmed, and although the outcome only justified their initial fears, the knowledge that nothing could or would be done about it probably gave them a certain grim pleasure.

His friendship with Len had been strained a bit in the end, but the odd stormy sea shouldn't worry a good crew, and Jack knew it would come good again, given time.

It was getting on dark when they left, so Jack slowly went down one step at a time to the street. He picked up the City Final from the lad on the corner near the station, before gingerly limping back to the office to pick up his overcoat before heading home.

As he opened the door and went over to his desk he sensed rather than heard the click of the hammer being drawn back, and turned slowly till he saw the black round hole that was just that bit darker than the surrounding gloom.

A grim voice hissed at him. "You're a focken dead mahn."

It was time to see if he'd lost any of his nerve. "Not again," he sighed." Can I ask why? Declan?"

"You're a focken cool one!"

"Well, I've faced death a few times before, mate. You just have to go with it."

"That's roit. You know who I am, so you know why . . . Say your prayers."

Jack measured his tone carefully. "I didn't do it."

"Oh, focken spare me."

He kept it level. "It's not a plea for mercy, sport, just the facts. I wish I had, to be honest, but I couldn't have."

"How so?"

"I just got out of hospital after five days lying on me face. I couldn't have been there."

He sensed a change in the air. "What were you doin' in there then?"

"A fucken madwoman took a divot outta me back with a shotgun. Do you want to see the mess they made stitching it up?"

The figure behind him exhaled, and Jack knew the gun was being lowered.

"Slowly does it, feller. Turn your lamp on there now."

He did as he was told; he couldn't have moved fast anyway.

The unshaven dark face had a blazing intensity as it materialised out of the darkness.

"Let's see it then."

Jack gingerly slid his shirt off his shoulder, grunting.

The Irishman peeled the bandage back roughly.

"Ow shit! Go easy."

"That's nasty, alright. A woman, you say? Did you fock her and leave her or somethin'?"

"I wouldna fucked her with your cock, mate. She was a monster, like the rest of her evil bloody family."

"Alright then, enough of that now. You're a cluey fella . . . So who killed me brother then, if not you?"

"They said he went in after a footy, didn't they? But you obviously don't think so, or you wouldn't be here waving that around at me."

The Irishman went pensive and sat down opposite him, laying the revolver on the desk between them – something Jack knew a man insecure about using firearms would never do.

"Me dad was a boatman. We grew up on the water. Both of us could swim before we even started school, and in some bloody wild water too. So you can't tell me he drowned in some focken little stream like you've got there. No fear. Some bugger . . ."

". . . Or buggers."

"Now that's a point you've got there. He was still a strong feller, even at his age."

"So what made you think it was me in the first place?"

"You were 'round that church like a bloody blowfly, and it's plain to see you're not a religious man . . . There was no one else upsetting him that I knew of."

"Think about it. Who stood to lose?"

"Lose from what?"

"The hanging coming out."

"What? That Communist feller? C'mon now, who gives a fock about that eejit?"

"Lots of people would have been up to their necks in shit if it'd all gone public, believe me. Bishops, rich men, top coppers, fucken all sorts . . . and a shady fucken crew they all are. I'll give ya the mail."

"Oi'll be focked! I never knew about all that."

"And here's somethin' else for the pot: last time our paths crossed . . ."

"When was that, then? Ye have the advantage of me."

"Seven or eight years back. You did a bank over in Alderley. I was one of the plods that rumbled ya."

"Were ya now? Oi would never've known."

"You had two grand on ya, no?"

"So I did."

"O'Reilly pocketed half."

"He did indeed. And yourself? "

"Yeah, well . . . so why didn't you say anything at the trial?"

"He was on our side, wasn't he?"

"What, with you lot?"

"Well so he said. And the money was to be goin' to the struggle."

"And did it?"

"Oi truly wonder, because no-one in my division knows anything about it. So that's something else I'll be lookin' into while I'm in the district. Back then O'Reilly just gave me a hundred to be goin' on with when I got out, and that was that. And naturally I got movin' very quickly; the rest of it's a mystery to this feller."

"You know him and your brother went back over twenty years. don't ya?"

"I never did, no."

"Well, they did. All the way back to that boy business."

"Ah, that . . . Now I can't say I approved of that, but family is family at the end of it, if you know what I mean."

"If you look at it like that . . . But think it through, mate. If your brother had cracked under the strain and blurted it all, who else might have gone down the plughole as well with them bishops and what have ya? It wouldna looked good."

"By me sainted mother . . . Focken O'Reilly."

"I never said a thing."

"You didn't have to."

The Irishman's brow furrowed as he struggled to bring out the next bit: "Oi'm sorry about nearly givin ya the chop, mind, but a death in the family can unsettle a man."

"Apology gratefully accepted, mate. But indulge me for a minute, will ya?"

He looked at his gun, then back at Munro. "Foir away."

"Speaking of family matters, if I may, how come your accent is as thick as bogwater, but your brother sounded like he was born here?"

"Ashamed he was of our humble beginnings, livin' from hand to mouth on a dirt floor. He trained himself to talk like whoever was higher up the chain than he was, always on the make. Me, I'm who I am, and fock you if ye don't like it."

He sat pensively for a moment, staring at the floor, then stood up.

"That's that then. You won't say you've seen me now, will ya?"

"Not if no one asks."

The Fenian laughed at that and pocketed the revolver as he went out the door.

Jack slowly sat back in his chair and realised he was bathed in sweat. It had been close. Bloody hell, too close. Another of the nine used up . . . how many were left?

23

The ocean sparkled with that special light it gets in late winter, and Aina was rugged up as she sat on the verandah. The house stood fairly isolated, but not too far from the shops at Burleigh. It was just a stroll to get the papers and such. The water wasn't too cold once you were in it and stayed out of the breeze. The best thing was, no bugger was about; they had the beach virtually to themselves, even on a warm day.

Jack had been out doing a bit of bodysurfing. He saw a bike against the fence as he came back over the dunes. The thin crust squeaked underfoot and set his teeth on edge, so he was glad to get to the gravel, even if it was tougher on his sea-softened feet. The telegram told him to ring a B. Mollinson at once. He towelled off and trotted down to the lone phone box at the end of the street, four coppers in his hand. Mollinson was a bookie, and the week before Jack had put fifty smackers on Spanish Princess in the last race at the next Doomben meet; it had come in at twenty to one.

Jack hadn't seen the papers to find out the results, so *Holy Moley! A grand!* and *You beauty!* was the cry . . . But there was a problem. Mollinson had overdone it on the day and taken a bath. He had no readies.

"Well where do we go from here, Molly me old mate?" he asked.

Mollinson thought for a bit. "You know, there's this other joker owed me roughly that much for a while now, so he's left me the deeds to a bit of land down near where yez are now. Bit north of there and back off the beach a bit. There's only one block on the water; the rest of it's sort of, you know, back a bit."

"What, fucken sandhills and sandflies?"

"Some of it's a bit low lying, but they reckon land prices in Surfer's Paradise are gunna go berko sooner rather than later, and that's just a piss an' a fart up the road."

"That fucken swamp?"

"Mate, they're gunna fill it in one day."

"So ya say . . . But how much of this land is usable, in the real sense, as in now? Can ya grow anything on it?"

"Not really. But it's a hundred acres, give or take a dunny run."

"Yeah, of shitbush and salty mud! The mozzies'd carry off a stud bull come summer!"

"Look, a bloke in the know told me to forget about the debt and hang on to the property – and he's richer than you and me and ten others besides. It might be a goer."

"I dunno. Bird in the hand, mate."

"Mate, a house at the beach has to be worth something. I'll chuck in a hundred cash so you can knock up a shack or somethin'. Ya won't regret it."

"Still not convinced. Let me sleep on it."

"Righto then. Ring us later."

He hung up and walked back, swinging his arms to try and loosen them up for another swim. Old Molly might have a point, but still: a grand is a grand.

He walked up the rickety steps and kissed Aina on the forehead. She was making a good recovery, but it looked like a no-no in the baby department. She was still troubled by it, and frequently broke down and cried. It would be a long haul, he could see, but he was getting a bit too old to be changing nappies anyway, as he kept telling her in an effort to cheer her up. Deep down he probably meant it too, tough as it was to accept.

He picked up the paper that had been delivered while he was in the water. An item on page three caught his eye.

POLICE INSPECTOR DIES IN ACCIDENT

Inspector Fergal O'Reilly of the Armed Hold-up Squad was killed yesterday when a hand grenade accidentally exploded. It was one of several that had been stolen from Army stores in Sydney some weeks ago.

An unknown informant had directed police to the stash of explosives, which they fear may have been intended for use in robberies. Sgt Brendan Mulvaney, 34, single, was also blinded in the accident. Enquiries are continuing as to the identity of the person who directed the officers to the hiding place.

It went on further about the terrible loss, blah blah blah, but Jack chuckled and put the paper down again. "His wonders to perform, eh love?" he said.

She looked at him with a puzzled frown and held out her hand.

He rubbed it and held it in both of his to warm it up as they sat together looking out at the surf.

Things could be worse.

GLOSSARY

This brief glossary of colloquial and underworld language inevitably includes words that refer to native Australian and immigrant ethnic groups in a derogatory and racist fashion. These are listed for reasons of social and historical accuracy, and their offensiveness is understood. Anyone interested in a more detailed resource for Australian slang should consult *The Macquarie Australian Slang Dictionary* (2004), or its predecessor, *The Macquarie Dictionary of Australian Colloquial Language*.

arc up : to become aggressive

ball-catchers : men's underwear

battler : a hard-up working person

Birdsville Track : legendary outback dirt highway that runs for over 500 km, mostly through desert, between southwest Queensland and northern South Australia

bludger : a layabout, originally one who lived off his woman's sexual earnings

boofhead : a term of affection or mild contempt (from popular 1940s Aussie cartoon character)

boong : derogatory term for Aboriginal Australians, used by non-Aboriginals

brekkie : breakfast (also *brekka*)

bumnuts : eggs

bundy on : to start work (from Bundy, a brand of workplace timekeeping clock with punch-cards, once ubiquitous (unrelated to the contemporary slang term for a brand of rum)

chippie : carpenter

chook : generic term for poultry; can also mean a stupid or awkward person

chuck : vomit, usually alcohol-induced

clippie : tram conductor

clobber : clothes ("good clobber" : one's best outfit, to wear when "going out")

cockatoo : lookout used in gambling or other illegal activities

cooee : high-pitched call used to communicate over distances in the bush

corrie : corrugated iron

damper : homemade bread, made without yeast

date : anus

deener : a shilling

drongo : a stupid or dull-witted person

the drum : the latest information, usually the 'real story' (*see also:* the mail)

durry : a cigarette, usually a hand-rolled one

Ekka : annual agricultural show held in Brisbane. Its official name is the Royal Queensland Show.but it is generally known as the Ekka, short for exhibition, after its original name, the Brisbane Exhibition

fairy floss : spun sugar on a stick, usually pink (US: cotton candy; UK: candy floss)

fizgig : a police informer

form guide : horse-racing section of the daily newspaper

gin : commonly used at the time to refer to an Aboriginal woman, now considered derogatory

gyppo : originally WW1 military slang term for an Egyptian, later applied generally to Mediterranean people, but now obsolete

horse's : a homosexual male (rhyming slang: horse's hoof = poof)

Jackie Howe : a blue singlet named after its inventor, a legendary 19th-century shearer

King's shilling : *to take the King's shilling* – to enlist in the army

knocking shop : brothel

largy : a long-neck bottle of beer

laughing clowns : rotating-head carnival machines with cheap prizes

lie doggo : to conceal onself, usually in order to to wait or observe

lobster : a £10 note, pinkish-red in colour

the mail: an update

Mater : Mater Misericordiae Hospital in Woolloongabba, Brisbane; run by nuns, originally a hospital for the poor

muddies : mudcrabs

neck-oil : beer

noggin : head

nong : fool

pimp : an informer or schoolyard tell-tale (unrelated to US meaning)

PMG : Postmaster-General; the government department in charge of telephone and postal services, until it was broken up in the 1970s

pony : a five-ounce glass of beer, much favoured in the outback in the days before advanced refrigeration

poo man : derogatory term for a homosexual male

poofy : flash or effete (not necessarily homosexual)

pot : a standard ten-ounce glass of beer, known in other states as a middy

Prods : Protestants, whose rivalry with Catholics was an important social divide at the time

quid : specifically, a one-pound note, but also used as a generic term for money

rozzers : cops

Salvos : the Salvation Army

sanger : sandwich

seppoes : Americans (rhyming slang: Yanks = septic tanks)

shanks's pony : walking

size tens : police boots

smalls : underwear

SP : (= starting price); illegal off-course betting on horse races, mostly run in pubs at the time

spiv : a con man or villain, notable for sharp clothes and/or ostentatious behaviour

Spring-heeled Jack : a legendary burglar in Victorian England; an extremely agile person.

stumps : the end of proceedings (the end of the day's play in cricket)

Tally-Ho : famous Aussie brand of cigarette papers

toast rack : the centre section of early trams; without doors for quick passenger boarding

two bob : two shillings; a two-shilling coin

urger : a low-life racetrack tipster, whose job is to drive odds up or down with rumours or gossip

wacko : a usually sarcastic term of amazement (unrelated to contemporary meaning of crazy)

wax vestas : old-style phosphor matches, packaged in a tin box with a roughened base for striking

ABOUT THE AUTHOR

G. S. Manson, former meat-packer,
barman, rock journalist, demolition
man, porno salesman, roller-disco
mechanic, and debt collector, now
divides his time between laying
down hypnotic funk grooves as
half of indigenous trance band
GURIGURU and trying to run an
organic pecan farm. He also has no
trouble walking the mean streets
of his own mind as a crime writer
with a uniquely Australian voice.